Blaze

Dear Reader,

St. Valentine's Day has always been one of my favorite holidays, and I thought it would be the perfect backdrop for my fifth Wrong Bed book. I love writing stories in which two people, who think they are so wrong for each other, discover (much to their initial horror) that they make a perfect match!

Special FBI agent Nicola Guthrie and Security expert Gabe Wilder share a common goal. They are each determined to catch a thief—namely the media celebrity who's been robbing Denver's socially elite and who only strikes on holidays.

With St. Valentine's Day a mere forty-eight hours away, the clock is ticking, and Nicola's prime suspect is Gabe. Of course, that doesn't stop her from falling into bed with him the first chance she gets...

For me Valentine's Day has always been about friendship as well as romance. So I hope you enjoy meeting Gabe's best friends, Nash and Jonah, and that you will look for their stories in July and December.

For more news about upcoming books, please visit my website, www.carasummers.com.

Happy Valentine's Day!

Cara Summers

Cara Summers

TAKE MY BREATH AWAY...

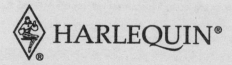

TORONTO • NEW YORK • LONDON
AMSTERDAM • PARIS • SYDNEY • HAMBURG
STOCKHOLM • ATHENS • TOKYO • MILAN • MADRID
PRAGUE • WARSAW • BUDAPEST • AUCKLAND

Recycling programs
for this product may
not exist in your area.

ISBN-13: 978-0-373-79597-0

TAKE MY BREATH AWAY...

Copyright © 2011 by Carolyn Hanlon

www.eHarlequin.com

Printed in U.S.A.

ABOUT THE AUTHOR

Was Cara Summers born with the dream of becoming a published romance novelist? No. But now that she is, she still feels her dream has come true. She loves writing for the Blaze line because it allows her to create strong, determined women and seriously sexy men who will risk everything to achieve *their* dreams. Cara has written more than thirty-five books for Harlequin Books, and when she isn't working on new stories, she teaches in the Writing Program at Syracuse University and at a community college near her home.

Books by Cara Summers

Don't miss any of our special offers. Write to us at the following address for information on our newest releases.

Harlequin Reader Service
U.S.: 3010 Walden Ave., P.O. Box 1325, Buffalo, NY 14269
Canadian: P.O. Box 609, Fort Erie, Ont. L2A 5X3

To all of my readers everywhere!
Thanks so much for your support.
Happy Valentine's Day!

Prologue

The day after Thanksgiving…

"I'M THINKING WHAT WE'VE got here is a copycat thief." FDI Agent Nick Guthrie kept his eyes steady on Gabe Wilder as he gestured to the Monet propped on the credenza to the left of his desk. In front of the cleverly forged painting lay a copy of that morning's *Denver Post*. The headline read: Priceless Monet Stolen on Thanksgiving Day.

"Don't you agree? He replaces the original with a very good copy. That's what your father always did. He's even signing your father's initials."

Gabe said nothing, letting the silence stretch between them. He'd been coming to grips with the fact that someone was imitating his father ever since Guthrie had called him to the crime scene the night before. At 6:30 a.m., the FBI offices were still empty, and Guthrie hadn't bothered to draw the shades on the glass walls that divided his office from the others in the White-Collar Crime Division.

"Well?" Guthrie prompted Gabe. "What are you thinking?"

"We're not dealing with a copycat." He shifted his gaze to the Monet.

"No?" Guthrie frowned. "The thief broke through one of the best security alarm systems available, one of yours. He has a detailed knowledge of the M.O. your father used. And it's a French Impressionist painting. Raphael Wilder was particularly talented at forging those. I say someone is deliberately imitating your father's style right down to signing the forgery with the initials, R.W."

"But my father never sent announcements bragging about his thefts," Gabe pointed out.

"Agreed," Guthrie said. "But everything else is the same."

Gabe couldn't argue with that. But why would someone choose to imitate the style of a legendary art thief and then deviate in a major way from his method? And why was this thief choosing to copy his father in the first place? Those were the questions that he intended to find the answers to.

"I had a chance to study the original painting when my company set up the security at the Langfords' house." Gabe nodded his head toward the Monet. "The forgery is a good one. It might have been years before the fake was detected."

Guthrie leaned back in his chair. "So why announce the theft?"

"Exactly. Raphael Wilder never would have." Then Gabe met Nick Guthrie's eyes. "That's why I'm not willing to agree that this thief is simply a copycat. There's more going on here. Why don't you come right out and ask *me* if I had something to do with stealing the Monet? The possibility must have crossed your mind. No one would know my father's methods better than I. His initials are on the painting. The Langfords were using *my* security system."

Guthrie said nothing.

"Perhaps I substituted the forgery when I installed the alarm system. That would eliminate the need to go back and break in later. I could sell the original and no one would be the wiser, perhaps ever."

"That's what your father would have done." Guthrie shot him a frown. "And maybe your involvement in the theft did cross my mind, but I dismissed the possibility. Raphael Wilder was a thief, a very good one, and if you'd followed in his footsteps, I imagine you'd have made a very good one also. But you haven't. We go back a long way, Gabe."

That much was true. The first day he'd met FBI Agent Nick Guthrie was the day the man had come into his home and arrested his father for grand larceny. That had been over fifteen years ago. And within a month of Raphael Wilder's conviction, he'd died in prison of pneumonia. Ever since then, Nick Guthrie had kept close tabs on Gabe. What might have begun as feelings of guilt or responsibility on Guthrie's part had evolved gradually into a friendship, one that ran both ways.

And Nick Guthrie had been one of the people who'd helped him stay on the straight and narrow at a time in his life when he might have chosen a different path. He owed other people, too, of course. Father Mike Flynn and the St. Francis Center for Boys had played a key role.

Nick Guthrie leaned forward. "I know about the promise you made your mother when she was dying. I was with you and Father Mike the day that you renewed that promise to your father in the prison infirmary. There's no way that you would break those vows by starting to steal paintings. You've built a business to protect people from theft and from harm. And you're doing a damn good job of it."

Gabe didn't smile, but the knot that had been in his stomach when Guthrie had asked him to come into the office that morning eased. If Nick Guthrie hadn't requested this meeting, Gabe would have insisted on one himself. He'd needed to know just how much G. W. Securities was going to come under suspicion because of his father.

Guthrie ran his hands through his hair. "Besides, if you were to take up a life of crime, I can't see you sending announcement cards. And why target one of your own security systems? I've known you since you were thirteen. You're not that dumb."

Now Gabe *did* smile. "So it really did cross your mind?"

Guthrie sighed. "Of course it did. I'm an FBI agent. I have to consider all the possibilities. But you didn't steal the Monet. And I'm not releasing any of the details about the thief using your father's M.O. to the press."

"Well, you're right about me, as it happens. I didn't steal the painting. But..."

Guthrie raised his hands, palms out. "I know. I know. You still think I was wrong about your father."

It was a discussion they'd had often over the years. Gabe was willing to admit that his father had been a thief, a brilliant one. And a reformed one. He'd never believed his father had stolen the Pissaro that Guthrie had arrested him for stealing. Raphael Wilder had denied the theft even on his deathbed. "My father made the same promise to my mother that I did. He didn't steal that painting."

Guthrie rose and walked to the window. Over the years they'd agreed to disagree. The first time they'd argued about his father's innocence, Gabe had punched the older man. He'd been thirteen and angry.

Guthrie had taken the punch and told him that he could take another. Anytime. But Gabe hadn't punched him again because it hadn't helped soothe any of the pain or the loss away. What had eventually helped was the time he'd spent at the St. Francis Center for Boys. At a crucial time in his life, Father Mike Flynn had helped him more than he could ever repay. Truth told, the priest was still helping him. He'd been the first person he'd called after he'd left the crime scene the night before.

"There was a time when I thought you might follow in your father's footsteps," Guthrie said. "But you've built a very different kind of life."

Yes, he had. And G. W. Securities was becoming known beyond Denver. Partly due to some consulting work he'd done for Nick Guthrie, he'd recently landed jobs as far away as D.C. and New York City. Gabe stretched out his legs and crossed them at the ankles.

"So why is someone imitating parts of your father's M.O.?" Guthrie spoke the question that was foremost in both of their minds.

As it hung unanswered in the air, Gabe's attention was distracted by the young woman who'd just stepped out of the elevator in the outer offices. Something moved through him as she strode purposefully toward a desk in one of the glass-walled offices and set her briefcase down.

Not recognition.

Or was it? He gave her another few seconds of his attention. There was plenty there to warrant a second look. The gray slacks and jacket did little to disguise the long legs and the curves in that neat, athletic body. The bright blue of the shirt drew his gaze to her face—also worth a second look.

This time he was sure it was recognition that flickered. He knew that short upturned nose, the stubborn chin.

"Who…?"

Gabe wasn't even aware that he'd spoken the question out loud until Guthrie answered, "That's Nicola, my daughter. She started working here a week ago."

Gabe registered the frown in the older man's voice, but he didn't take his gaze off of the woman.

"She didn't even tell Marcia and me that she was applying to the FBI, not until she'd been accepted at Quantico. She finished her training there last month and received the Director's Leadership Award. I had to pull a lot of strings to get her transferred here."

Nicola Guthrie. Of course. It was the hair that had thrown him. Now it fell straight as rain until it curved beneath her chin. Fifteen years ago a mass of curls had framed her face. He'd teased her ruthlessly about them and even pulled them a few times.

"I'm going to limit her to research on this case," Guthrie was saying. "She's smart, but she's not ready for field work. As long as she's in the office and behind that desk, I can be sure she's safe."

Gabe was about to turn his attention back to the Monet when Nicola Guthrie turned and her gaze suddenly locked on his.

The impact ricocheted through his system, coming into contact with every nerve ending. For a moment he couldn't breathe. Everything else faded, and all he was aware of was her. The sudden tightening in his gut was raw, sexual and compelling. Without any conscious volition, he rose from the chair.

"Gabe?"

Guthrie's voice came from a distance. Still, the sound might have been the only thing that allowed him to keep his feet firmly planted on the floor. The urge to go to her was so intense. He'd never felt a pull that strong. He couldn't drag his gaze away from her. He felt trapped. But he couldn't seem to summon up the will to fight his desire.

"What is it?" Guthrie's voice was closer now. Gabe felt

Guthrie's hand on his arm. But it wasn't until Nicola turned away that he was able to draw in a breath. Or gather a coherent thought.

"What's wrong?" Guthrie asked.

"It's this case." Gabe was surprised to find his voice worked. He was still looking at her as she picked up a file and leafed through it.

What the hell *was* wrong with him? No woman had ever affected him this way before. All that had happened was that their eyes had met. She was standing a good twenty-five feet away and she'd made him feel weak, winded.

What would she do to him when she was closer? When he kissed her? When he touched her? When he was inside of her?

No.

Ruthlessly, Gabe reined his thoughts in and turned to face the man he called a friend. "I want some answers. I don't have any idea why someone is using parts of my father's M.O." But there was a reason. He was sure of it.

"The announcement cards are easier," he continued. "This particular thief craves attention. Which means that he may strike again to get more."

"I wish we weren't thinking along the same lines," Guthrie said in a grim tone. "That brings me to the reason I asked you to come in today. I figure you're going to be working on this case and I'd like you to agree to share any information you come up with. My office will do the same. What do you say?"

Gabe managed a smile as he held out a hand. "I say two heads are always better than one."

Guthrie glanced toward the painting again. "I hope that we're both wrong about another robbery."

Gabe hoped so, too. But his gut told him they weren't.

As he left the FBI offices, he noted that more people had

reported to work. And in spite of his determination not to, he glanced once more in the direction of Nicola Guthrie's office.

Her head was bent over a file.

Gabe wasn't sure it was relief or disappointment he felt as the elevator doors closed and he descended to the street level.

1

Two and a half months later, February 12

"TURN LEFT IN point nine miles."

The calm voice of her GPS system had FBI special agent Nicola Guthrie gripping the steering wheel of her car and peering through the windshield into thickly falling snow. Easing her foot off the gas, she narrowed her eyes to study what lay in the beams of her headlights.

Not much. She was finding it more and more difficult to distinguish the narrow mountain road from the treacherous ditches that bordered it on either side.

The storm had been steadily increasing in intensity ever since she'd left Denver at 6:00 p.m. And her little Volkswagen Beetle convertible was not known for its winter weather capabilities. The one-hour drive to the church of St. Francis had stretched into nearly three.

And counting.

But it was going to be worth it. The moment that Father Mike Flynn had walked into her office and showed her the note, she'd gotten that tingling feeling deep inside of her—the same one that had guided every important decision she'd ever made. And it had never failed her.

Tonight, she had a good chance of finally identifying the art thief who'd been leading the FBI on a merry chase for the past three months. On each holiday since Thanksgiving, he'd relieved one of Denver's art collectors of a priceless painting. And if she unmasked him tonight, her father would finally have to relent and take her career choice seriously.

Nicola glanced at her speedometer. She could walk faster than this.

"Turn left in point five miles."

Not much longer. Her decision to join the FBI had not set well with either her father or her stepmother. Her father's tendency to be over-protective she could understand. Her mother had been an agent who'd worked with him, and she'd died in the line of duty when Nicola had been a toddler.

Her stepmother was a different kettle of fish. Marcia Thorne Guthrie had been born to wealth, and her ideas about a woman's role in society were slightly and almost lovably medieval. Marcia thought women should study art and literature, marry, run a lovely home and spread her largesse through the community by doing good works. *And* by throwing huge charity balls like the one Marcia gave every year at Thorne Mansion on Valentine's Day.

In fact, that's exactly where Nicola should be right now—at Thorne Mansion helping her stepmother make the final dessert selections for the ball.

The problem was Nicola didn't want to follow in her stepmother's footsteps. She wanted to follow in her father's. But she dearly loved both of her parents—enough to get a Masters in Fine Art degree before she'd secretly applied to the FBI. Throughout her life, her rebellions against her parents had ended in eventual victories, but they had always been hard-won. And actions had always spoken louder than words. Eventually, she'd win them over.

Which was why tonight was so important. If she could just catch herself a thief… And if that thief turned out to be who she thought it was? Well, her father would have to give her bonus points for that because he thought Gabe Wilder was as innocent as a newborn babe.

She didn't.

"Turn left in point three miles."

"Where?" Nicola frowned into the swirling snow.

Then she saw it—just the outline of the church steeple. Ahead and to her left. She might have missed it if not for the headlights of a vehicle parked nearby. When a sudden break in the wind gave her a better look at the silhouette of the parked car, Nicola's pulse jumped.

It was an SUV and it looked familiar. Could it be…?

The tingling sensation moved through her. She'd felt the same way when Father Mike had visited her office and shown her the note announcing that the statue of St. Francis was going to be stolen tonight. Gabe Wilder might very well be here.

"Turn left in one hundred yards."

One step at a time, Nicola. First, you have to find the driveway. Then the thief.

During the long drive from the city, her practical side had been cautioning her that a semi-retired Franciscan priest like Father Mike didn't fit the profile of the previous wealthy and socially prominent victims of Denver's well-publicized art thief. However, during the twenty years he'd served as the director of the St. Francis Center for Boys, Father Mike had certainly rubbed elbows with the movers and shakers of Denver.

And the thief always delivered a note to his next target

on the day he struck. Father Mike had received his note today. She'd read it.

I've always admired the statue of St. Francis—ever since I first saw it in the prayer garden at the St. Francis Center. I was so disappointed when you moved it to that isolated church. So, I've decided to take it off your hands. Enjoy Lincoln's Birthday.

The bragging tone and the specificity of the note were similar to the other ones in the file. The art piece and the holiday were always mentioned by name.

No one had expected the thief to make a move on Lincoln's Birthday, February 12. The press, the FBI and most of Denver's socially elite were expecting the thief to strike on Valentine's Day. A priceless Cézanne was going to be auctioned at the annual Valentine's Day Charity Ball—the one her stepmother was throwing—and the theory was that the thief wouldn't be able to resist it.

No one had given any thought to the possibility that the thief might target the statue of St. Francis. Truth told, she hadn't thought of it either. She'd been certain her father was right, and the thief would go after the Cézanne.

The small marble statue currently residing on a side altar in St. Francis Church didn't have the monetary value of the artwork previously stolen. But there were those who would testify that it was priceless.

The statue of St. Francis had been donated to the Franciscan order in Denver years ago by an immigrant family from Assisi, Italy. They'd claimed it had been sculpted in the image of the saint himself, and that it possessed special powers to grant prayers. Since its arrival in Denver, the reputation of the statue had grown to legendary proportions. Even in its original home in the small prayer garden next to the St. Francis Center for Boys, the statue had attracted crowds. Many thought that paying a visit to the statue and saying a prayer was like having a direct line to God.

There were no documented miracles. Yet. But there were plenty of people who'd testified to the fact that the prayers they'd said to the statue had not only been answered but had changed their lives. People had fallen in love, marriages had been saved and babies had been born to supposedly infertile couples. And almost everyone testified to finding peace.

The article published in last Sunday's edition of the *Denver Post* had included several of the stories. They ranged from recovering lost jewelry to improvements in health and relationships. There was even a local congresswoman who claimed she owed her latest election victory to St. Francis.

Nicola remembered a time when she'd believed in the power of the statue herself. She'd said a prayer, one she'd desperately wanted to be granted. But St. Francis hadn't been listening that day. She hadn't wasted another prayer on him since. But she was definitely in the minority.

When the St. Francis Center for Boys had been torn down and replaced by upscale townhomes as part of the city's urban renewal program, Father Mike had received permission to relocate the statue to St. Francis Church. Since then the pilgrimages to pray to the statue had picked up in numbers.

Nearly half the money that had sustained the St. Francis Center had come from visitors who'd left donations in the small prayer garden where the statue had stood for fifteen years. Currently the three masses Father Mike commuted to say on Sunday were packed, and at least twenty percent of attendees were people from out of state who'd come to say a prayer.

What was the value of a piece of art that could answer

your prayers? Nicola figured it might bring in a hefty price from some collector.

Evidently enough to have Father Mike hiring G. W. Securities, the premier firm in Denver, to protect it at its new location. That little known fact had also received quite a bit of play in the *Denver Post* article.

So if the statue of St. Francis was stolen, it would be the fourth piece of art snitched while under the protection of G. W. Securities. And to Nicola's way of thinking that made the company's owner, Gabe Wilder, a prime suspect. The fact that Gabe was the son of legendary thief Raphael Wilder added more weight to her suspicions.

"Turn left in twenty-five yards."

As Nicola peered into the snow, a blast of wind slammed into her car and the rear wheels fishtailed. Holding her breath, she eased her foot off the gas and kept her hands steady on the wheel. Her headlights shifted, briefly pinning the SUV, and Nicola's pulse jumped again. That was Gabe Wilder's car all right.

This time the tingling feeling racing through her was so strong that she nearly trembled. Then she felt her tires regain traction, and she shifted her attention to the road.

Her suspicion that Gabe Wilder had to be playing a key role in the thefts was the reason she'd spent the past few weeks tailing that SUV all over Denver during her off duty hours. Not that her surveillance had done her any good. Thanks to secure underground parking garages and the fact that he lived in an apartment above his office, she hadn't even been able to get a good look at the man himself.

Still, Nicola couldn't rid herself of her gut feeling that Gabe had to be connected to the thefts. Each time she'd tried to connect the dots in the case, he was the one who triggered that tingling sensation.

Beneath her, she felt her tires spin and slide to the right.

Focus, Nicola. When she peered through the windshield all she could see in the glare of her headlights was a whirling tunnel of snow. But the driveway to the church had to be close. The GPS lady was never wrong. She pressed her foot lightly against the brake. Surely that SUV would have left tracks. Any minute now she'd see the indentations in the snow. She slowed some more. But if she made a left turn without being sure, she'd end up in the ditch.

"Recalculating," her GPS system chirped.

"Damn." She'd missed the driveway, but at least she hadn't gone off the road. Not yet.

"Drive point four miles to Balfour Road."

"In your dreams," Nicola muttered as she eased her car to what she thought was the side of the road and stopped. That was when she saw the other vehicle. It was about fifteen yards ahead of her, just at the end of where her headlights reached. And it was tilting to one side in the ditch she'd been trying so hard to avoid.

Hoping that she'd left enough room for any possible travelers to get by her, she turned off the engine and then studied the other not-so-lucky car in her headlights. It was completely covered in snow, so it was impossible to figure the make or model—or even the color. It looked as if it had been abandoned. Just to make sure, she pressed the heel of her hand on her horn and gave three sharp blasts.

Nothing.

The church would be the closest refuge. She grabbed a flashlight out of her glove compartment, tucking it into the pocket of her coat. Then she turned up her collar and opened the driver's door. Fighting the wind, she climbed out.

Her first surprise was that the snow almost came up

to her knees. The second was the force of the wind that pushed her back against the car. Nicola shoved her hair back and managed to get the door closed.

Reaching the church ASAP had to be her first priority. Gabe Wilder had left his headlights on, which made it easier for her to see through the darkness. Assuming that *was* Gabe Wilder's SUV, he had to be here because of the statue. And she couldn't discount the possibility that whoever had been driving that abandoned car was inside with him. If one of them was the thief, that didn't bode well for the other.

She shifted her gun from her holster to her coat pocket for easy access and moved forward.

2

HE WASN'T ALONE in the church.

Gabe had sensed that from the moment he'd found the door unlocked and the security alarm disabled. His conviction had grown steadily during the time it had taken him to walk quietly up the aisle to the side altar.

Since the storm had taken the power out, the place was as dark and cold as a crypt. The only illumination was provided by the three-tiered stand of votive lights in front of the altar. Nowadays, people didn't light real candles. Instead they donated money to purchase lights powered by lithium batteries. And they "burned" brightly enough for him to see that the statue of St. Francis was still there, enclosed in a shatterproof glass dome.

Inwardly, Gabe grinned. Turnabout was fair play. And very satisfying. The guy who'd had such smooth sailing so far must be feeling at least some of the frustration he'd been feeling for the past three months. There was no duplicate of the security system he'd created for the statue, not even a prototype out there, because he'd just invented it. It was very difficult to crack a safe or break through a security system when one had nothing to practice on.

Gabe started up the short flight of steps to the altar.

It was only as he reached the top that he saw it—the second statue sitting in the shadows at the foot of the altar. Crouching down, he examined it in the dim light, running his hands over it just to be sure. Then he welcomed the pump of adrenaline. It was a copy of the St. Francis, and that had to mean that his instincts had been right. The thief was still here.

Where?

In spite of the fact that all of his senses were now on full alert, Gabe was careful to keep the expression on his face perfectly neutral as he rose, narrowed his eyes and pretended to study the St. Francis that still stood beneath the glass dome.

The trap he'd set had worked. It was Father Mike who'd first suggested the idea that he might use the statue as bait, and the more Gabe had thought it over, the more he'd wanted to try it out. He'd called a friend at the *Denver Post,* and the resulting article in last Sunday's paper had not only highlighted the "priceless" reputation the statue had always had for answering prayers, but it had also mentioned that G. W. Securities had designed a premier alarm system for its protection. Evidently the combination of information had lured the thief into planning an attempt on the statue, just as he'd hoped.

The timing had surprised him. It was still two days until Valentine's Day, and the press as well as the law enforcement agencies had been expecting the thief to strike then. But the moment that Father Mike had called to tell him about the note, he'd sent the priest to the FBI office to update Nick Guthrie and he'd rushed up here.

Now, with the statue's help...

He mentally said a prayer, and then he just listened. There was nothing but the muted howling of the storm outside. His eyes had fully adjusted to the dim light, and he saw nothing in his peripheral vision that seemed out of place in the shadows.

His guess was that the thief had found a place to hide. His gaze went immediately to the door of the choir loft. It was open. Slipping quietly away from the altar, he moved along the side wall of the church until he reached the door.

For a moment, he paused and listened hard.

Nothing.

Then he heard it, the scrape of wood against wood, and he felt a draft of icy cold air. Pushing through the door, he ran into the room.

The blow caught him by surprise. Pain exploded in his head and icy water poured down the collar of his shirt. With stars spinning in front of his eyes, he stepped to the side and the kick aimed for his groin glanced off his thigh.

Off balance, he threw himself forward and took his opponent to the ground. They rolled across the marble floor, each struggling for an advantage. A table overturned and glass shattered. He was on the bottom when their bodies slammed into a wall.

Hands closed around his throat and cut off his air. Vision blurring, Gabe gripped his attacker's waist and bucked upward. The hands loosened around his throat, and Gabe reared up and butted heads with his opponent. Pain zinged through his skull, but it did the trick. He was suddenly free.

Scrambling up, he ran after his opponent. He would have been successful if his feet hadn't suddenly shot right out from beneath him. He fell backward, heard the crack as his head struck a counter. Then another explosion of pain blacked out everything.

NICOLA DUCKED HER HEAD and fought her way into the wind. Icy pellets stung her skin, and the boots that had been entirely appropriate for a day in the Denver office were no match for the snow that came closer to her knees as she moved forward.

Using her hand to shield her eyes, she checked on the SUV's location and adjusted her course. The headlights of the parked vehicle were all she could see now and they were helpfully aimed toward the long flight of steps that led to the front door of the church.

Everything else was totally engulfed in darkness and snow. When she reached the SUV, she leaned against it for a moment to catch her breath. Then she checked the license plate.

She felt a lot more than a tingle now. This confirmed it was Gabe Wilder's car. The plate numbers were as familiar to her as the details of the file she'd been compiling on him for nearly three months. She'd been right. From the first moment her dad had assigned her to gather research on the case, she'd been sure that Gabe had to be involved.

It wasn't just the fact that the thief was using his father's M.O., nor that Gabe's firm had handled the security for each victim. There was something about Gabe Wilder that just...fit. She knew what it was like to want desperately to follow in your father's footsteps—and to have to sometimes disguise that desire. But a person couldn't do that forever.

Just then the headlights went off. Was it one of those models where that happened automatically? Just to make sure...she felt her way along the side of the vehicle and pulled open the driver's door.

Empty.

He had to be in the church. Circling around the SUV, she pulled out her flashlight and headed toward the stairs. Finally, she was going to have a face-to-face meeting with Gabe Wilder, and she had no idea what he looked like. At least not anymore. The last time she'd seen him he'd been thirteen and she'd been ten.

As she gripped the iron railing and started up the long flight of stone steps, she let her mind return to those six months of her life when her stepmother had taken her every Saturday to the St. Francis Center. Charitable works were high on Marcia Thorne Guthrie's list.

The St. Francis Center had been located in a brick store-front building in downtown Denver. The first time she'd seen Gabe, she'd been standing in the small prayer garden that sat like a tiny oasis between the main building and a fenced in basketball court. He'd been tall with longish dark hair and scruffy jeans, and he'd had bad boy written all over him. At first he'd totally ignored her as he'd dribbled, jumped and sent the ball flying through the hoop again and again and again.

It had been Father Mike's idea for her to weed the garden while Marcia shelved donated books in the library. But she'd never gotten to the weeds. She hadn't been able to take her eyes off of Gabe Wilder.

Of course, she'd read all about his father, the notorious art thief, and how he'd died in prison. And she'd overheard her father speak about Gabe—about how hurt and angry he was. She'd known that he was at the center so that Father Mike could save him.

That's what Father Mike did—he saved bad boys. Most of the ones who came to the center shared Gabe's reputation. They came from all walks of life—some from the streets, some from the wealthiest Denver families—but as Marcia had put it: "Until they came to Father Mike, they were trouble with a capital *T*."

And that was exactly what Gabe Wilder had appeared to be. Trouble. She could see the anger and recklessness in the way he handled the ball. But she could also see a passion for the game. And it fascinated her. He fascinated her.

Suddenly he'd turned to face her. "What are you staring at?"

Nicola recalled that she'd swallowed hard and finally managed to blurt out, "You."

Bouncing the ball, he'd moved a few steps closer. "Why?"

A part of her knew that she shouldn't even be talking to him. She should be weeding. But she hated gardening and basketball looked like it would be so much more fun.

She drew in a deep breath and let it out. "Because you're great at basketball."

He turned and sent the ball whooshing through the hoop. Then he turned back to her. "You know how to play?"

"No." Basketball was not on Marcia's list of approved activities. Painting lessons, piano, ballet—those were.

To her utter amazement and delight, he'd sent the ball twirling on the tip of his finger. "I could teach you."

"No, I—I couldn't..." She knew very well that her stepmother hadn't brought her here to play basketball with one of the center's boys. But something in his eyes was tempting her, daring her.

"Why not?" he asked.

Why not indeed? It wasn't as though her stepmother was here watching her. And she did want to play. So much.

He bounced the ball again. "Look," he'd said, impatience clear in his tone. "I got friends coming in an hour. Want to shoot a few or not?"

Nicola could still recall the tingling sensation that had streamed through her whole body as she'd raced through the garden gate and onto the court.

"Ready?" Gabe had asked.

And when she'd nodded, he'd tossed her the ball.

After that, she'd played basketball with him every Saturday morning for an hour before his friends Nash and Jonah had shown up. That was always when Father Mike had come out to call her back into the center.

When Marcia had discovered what had been going on, she hadn't been pleased. Basketball was a boys' game. But Nicola hadn't ever regretted those Saturdays. Gabe had teased her, tormented her and endlessly critiqued her game. But she'd learned. Playing basketball had been her first rebellion against the kind of woman Marcia wanted to mold her into. In an odd way, she owed Gabe Wilder, she supposed. If it hadn't been for him, she might never have found the courage to take a stand in high school and try out for the basketball team.

Who knew? If it hadn't been for Gabe, she might not have rebelled against Marcia's and her father's wishes even further and become an FBI agent.

Having finally reached the top of the church steps, Nicola stepped into a portico that partially shielded her from the force of the wind. She hadn't seen Gabe Wilder for more than fifteen years—in spite of the fact that her last act on leaving the St. Francis Center for Boys had been to say a quick prayer to St. Francis that she would.

Some prayers went unanswered, and some bad boys couldn't be saved.

She'd just reached the door of the church when she heard it. A crash? It was muffled by the wind, but Nicola was certain she'd heard something. Glass shattering? She recalled the picture in the *Denver Post* of the statue of St. Francis standing in its supposedly shatter-proof glass dome.

As she pulled out her gun, she ran her flashlight over the door and saw that it stood ajar. After slipping through the narrow opening, she paused again. There was illumination that wasn't coming from her flashlight. Candles. She spotted the blur of light at the front of the church to her left.

She'd barely taken two steps up the center aisle when she heard another noise. This time there was no doubt about it—glass shattering.

After pocketing her flashlight, Nicola raised her gun and raced forward. As she neared the front of the church, she thought she spotted movement near those candles on the side altar. Then she saw it—a shadowy silhouette standing in front of the altar, its hands outstretched.

"Stop." She gripped her gun with both hands as she cut around the front row of pews. "FBI. Raise your hands."

A body rammed into her and she fell, landing backside first on the floor, then sliding into the first row of pews. Her head cracked against the wood and for a second, all she saw was stars.

"Stop." She scrambled to her feet and raced down the aisle after the fleeing shadow. Without breaking stride, she raised her gun again and steadied it with her other hand. "Stop or I'll shoot."

He kept on running.

She fired her weapon just as the darkness swallowed the shadow. Sprinting after him, she reached the front door of the church just in time to hear the motor of the SUV rev up. Then it lurched forward.

She ran out onto the front steps. As the wind whipped her breath away, she gripped her gun in both hands and took aim, but the tail lights dimmed as the vehicle gained speed. Then even those vanished into the falling snow.

A mix of anger and disappointment welled inside of her as she lowered her weapon. More than anything, she wanted to fight her way back to her car. But there was no way she could give chase. Not in this kind of weather. Even in that SUV, Gabe Wilder would be a lucky man if he could drive down off the mountain without spinning into a ditch.

But at least this time, she had proof that he'd been at the scene of the crime. He was connected to the thefts all right. She had to fill her father in. Pulling out her cell phone, she glanced at the time. Nine-fifteen—barely ten minutes since she'd left her car.

And the signal was dead. She looked back at the open door of the church. Hopefully, there was a landline inside. Wilder might deny being here, but she'd have more than a gut feeling when she talked to her father this time, and he'd have to listen to her.

And Gabe Wilder would have some explaining to do. She'd identified herself as FBI and he hadn't stopped.

Suddenly, Nicola frowned. Of course, she could only accuse Gabe Wilder of leaving a crime scene *if* there'd been a crime.

Hunching her head against the wind, she fought her way back to the open church door. Once inside, she pulled it shut, locked it and reholstered her gun.

She located a light switch, but nothing came on when she flipped it. Not surprising. The storm must have knocked out the power lines. That had to be why it was so cold. The moment she turned her flashlight on, she could see her breath in the frigid air.

She hurried toward the side altar. The statue of St. Francis was still there, standing on the narrow altar completely enclosed in a glass case just as it had appeared in the photo. So that hadn't been what she'd heard breaking.

Then she felt it—a prickling at the back of her neck telling her that she was not alone in the church. Pulling out her gun, she turned, listening hard as she scanned the shadowy darkness behind her. But Gabe Wilder couldn't have come back. Not this fast. And she'd locked the door.

Keeping her gun at the ready, she ran the beam of her flashlight over the floor. No sign of broken glass. It wasn't until she climbed to the top step of the altar that she spotted the second statue, and her heart skipped a beat.

After setting her gun and her flashlight down, she lifted it and set it on the altar. Then she picked up her weapon and ran the beam of light over both statues. They seemed to match perfectly. Both carved in beautiful Italian marble. The would-be thief had brought along an excellent forgery, but instinct had her gaze returning to the one under the glass dome. She was betting that one was the real deal. Though she hadn't seen it in over fifteen years, there was the same look on its face, the one that lured you into trusting...

Nicola gathered her thoughts. She still hadn't found any broken glass—or any explanation for the sounds she'd heard when she'd first entered the church. Turning away from the statue, she raised her gun, and moved away from the altar. No sign of glass anywhere. A brief fan of her flashlight showed a door along the side wall.

She moved toward it. The cold blast of air hit her just as she spotted the boots. Work boots, well worn on the soles and scuffed on the toes. As she stepped into the room, her flashlight caught the rest of him, and her stomach knotted. The man was sprawled full-length on the hard marble floor.

And he wasn't moving.

3

As she dropped to her knees next to the man, Nicola absorbed other details. His legs were long and clad in black jeans. She noted the narrow waist, broad chest and shoulders. He wore a black T-shirt and an open Paul Bunyan-style plaid flannel shirt. It was rolled halfway up muscular forearms.

His face was cast in shadow. But the beam of her flashlight caught pale skin, dark hair, a strong nose and chin, a slash of cheekbones.

Recognition flickered at the edge of her mind, then faded when she saw the nasty-looking gash on the side of his forehead. Blood had already pooled on the marble floor beneath his head.

Nicola's stomach knotted again. His skin was too pale, his body too still. Setting down her gun, she balanced her flashlight to point upward. Then she slipped her hand beneath the collar of the plaid shirt and felt for a pulse.

She found one.

As it pushed strong and steady against her fingers, she let out a breath she hadn't even known she was holding. Whoever he was, he was still alive. And someone had worked hard to bring him down. The man was big. But his skin was cold and clammy.

And wet. So was his shirt. So were her slacks, for that matter. Then she noted for the first time the shards of broken glass and the flowers—a spray of red roses that lay strewn across the marble floor. The blood that had pooled around his head and shoulders was mixed with water from the broken vase.

Who was he? A janitor? The driver of that other car? Had he surprised Gabe Wilder when he was trying to steal the statue? But now wasn't the time to deal with any of those questions. When she glanced at him again, she once more felt a flicker of recognition, but she couldn't quite remember.

His cut needed attention. And if she didn't want him to go into shock, she was going to have to find a way to keep him warm.

Nicola took off her coat and tucked it as best she could around the unconscious man. It barely reached his knees. She slipped out of her suit jacket and pulled her silk T-shirt over her head. Folding it carefully into a square, she pressed it to the cut on the side of his forehead.

Finally, she placed her free hand on the side of his face and leaned closer. "Hey, can you hear me?"

No response.

She patted her palm firmly against his cheek. "You're going to be all right."

At least she was praying he would be.

Reaching for his hand, she drew it onto his chest and covered it with her own. Not an easy job. His palm was much larger than hers, his fingers long. They might have belonged to an artist, a pianist perhaps, except the backs of those long fingers were callused.

And they were cold. So was she. The draft of air she'd

felt when she'd first entered the room was growing more frigid by the second. Glancing around, she spotted the open window and scrambled up to close it. Then she returned to her knees beside the injured man and took his hand again. Squeezing his fingers, she raised her voice. "Can you hear me?"

His eyelids fluttered. She noticed for the first time how dark his lashes were, how long.

"Come on. Open your eyes."

He did. For an instant, as his gaze locked on hers, the punch of awareness and the flare of heat in her belly stole her breath away.

She'd seen this man before. He'd been in her father's office on the day after Thanksgiving. And he'd had the same effect on her then. Even through a glass wall, even at a distance of twenty-five feet, she'd felt the impact of his gaze like a punch. He'd made her lose track of everything.

"Cur...?"

The sound was little more than a gasp. *Cur?* It made no sense to Nicola. But it allowed her to shove the memory away and focus her attention on the injured man. She drew in a breath and felt her lungs burn.

"Head...hurts..." His fingers linked with hers and tightened.

This time when she met his eyes, she checked to see whether or not they were dilated. They weren't. Even in the dim light from her flashlight, she could distinguish clearly between the pinpoint of black at the center and the cloudy gray of his irises.

Then his lids drifted shut.

"Does it hurt anywhere else?" she asked. She had to find that out. And it was much safer to concentrate on that task than on what she'd just felt. Or what she'd felt that day in the FBI office.

But in the three months since it had happened, she hadn't been able to rid her mind of the memory. From the moment she'd walked into the office she'd been aware of him, but it hadn't been until his eyes had met hers that he'd registered fully on her senses.

And he'd registered *fully* all right. She was sure the impact might have been caught on a Richter scale—if there'd been one handy. Part of what she was feeling, she'd recognized—that tingling sensation that always told her something was just...somehow right.

But it had made no sense and it had never before made her feel as if the ground were dissolving beneath her feet. Not that she'd been able to feel her feet. All she could feel was him. And she'd wanted to feel more of him. Heat, glorious waves of it, had washed through her system. Every cell in her body had melted and yearned.

And when he'd risen to his feet in one fluid movement and taken a step toward her, she'd nearly run to him. Right through glass walls like some kind of superhero. The impulse had been so baffling, so totally insane, so verging on the irresistible that she'd finally found the strength to drag her gaze away from him.

And she couldn't, she wouldn't let him affect her that way again. Closing her eyes, she pulled in air, felt the burn in her lungs and then exhaled, and breathed in again.

Mental list time. When she opened her eyes, she checked the cut first and saw that the bleeding was slowing. After replacing the square of cloth, she slipped her fingers behind his head to check the back. The instant she touched the bump, he winced and made a sound.

So he'd suffered a double whammy to his head. No wonder he was woozy. Shifting her coat aside, she ran her hands on a quick journey from the back of his neck, down his arms. When he neither winced nor yelped again, she drew her palms from his shoulders to his waist, then from his hips down those long, long legs. The man was one solid wall of muscle.

And she still wanted him. There was no mistaking the heat that had flared to life deep inside of her as she'd run her hands over him. No controlling it, either. She knew what she was feeling. She wasn't stupid, so she'd pegged it the first time she'd seen him. Lust. Pure and simple. And incredibly intense.

Whoever believed that lightning couldn't strike twice was dead wrong. But wherever the lust had come from, it could just go back there. She had a job to do—a possible thief fleeing down a mountain, an injured man who was sliding into shock and two statues of St. Francis. Her plate was currently full.

She glanced down to where her hands still rested on his ankles. First step—she had to stop touching him. Releasing her grip, she was about to get to her feet when a sudden thought occurred to her. When she'd patted him down, she hadn't felt a wallet. But she checked his pockets just to make sure. She located a cell phone, but nothing else.

Had Gabe Wilder taken this man's wallet? Why?

She glanced back at his face. His eyes were closed now, and he looked even paler. She had questions, but he was in no condition to answer.

Fishing in her coat pocket, she located her cell and tried again.

Nothing.

Then she stared at the time. Nearly nine-thirty. Rising, she glanced around the small room and spotted the landline on a counter. There was no dial tone when she lifted the receiver. Even if she'd been able to call 911, it would take help some time to arrive. So she was on her own.

Grabbing some candles she found next to the phone,

she lit them. Then she located a pile of linen towels and mopped up the water around his head and shoulders. Finally, she dropped to her knees and took his hand again. It was so cold. "It's all right," she murmured. "You're going to be all right." As if to reassure herself of that, she lifted her square of T-shirt again and checked the cut. It was clean and not very deep. "You probably won't need stitches, and the bleeding has nearly stopped."

And she doubted he heard a word she was saying. But when she tried to pull her hand away, his grip tightened again—as if she were his lifeline.

"Statue..." he murmured.

"It's still here," she said.

"Both...?"

"They're both here." Curious about how much he'd seen, she leaned closer. "What happened?"

He didn't answer her this time, and a second later his hand went limp in hers. She felt the instant surge of panic and shoved it down. The steady rise and fall of his chest beneath their joined hands assured her that he was still with her.

For the moment.

"It's going to be all right. It's going to be all right."

And it was. It had to be. Step number one was to get him warm.

Shivering, she slipped back into the jacket she'd discarded earlier and buttoned it up; then she tucked her coat around him again. There had to be something in the closet that she could use to keep him warm.

Behind the first door she opened, she found choir robes hanging on hooks. Though they were a different color, they reminded her of the robe that St. Francis wore in the sculpture. She thought of the statue's special prayer-answering powers. In spite of the fact that she'd tried praying to him once before without much success, she decided to give him a second chance.

"Help me keep him safe and well until I can get him medical attention," she murmured. Then she started pulling robes off their hangers.

GABE STRUGGLED TO FIND his way to the surface again. He'd done it once, hadn't he? Or had he just dreamed that he'd seen Curls leaning over him?

Focus.

His thoughts were spinning like little whirlpools—just out of reach. There was something important, something he needed to take care of. The statue…the effort it took to remember had pain stabbing his head again.

Okay. For a moment, he gave up, letting himself drift. And he saw her again.

Curls.

The moment her image took shape in his mind, his headache eased, and the memory slid into place. He let himself drift with it. He'd been at the St. Francis Center shooting baskets, and he'd sensed someone watching him. Not his friends, Nash and Jonah, who never made it to the center until noon. And sure enough, there she'd stood in the small garden beside the basketball court, her hands wrapped around the narrow poles in the wrought-iron fence. She'd looked like a prisoner. Perhaps that's what had appealed to him, what had triggered a sense in him that they were kindred spirits.

Because at that time, he'd felt like a prisoner, too, trapped in promises that he wasn't sure he wanted to keep. He'd stood beside his mother's bed holding his father's hand as they'd both sworn their vows. He'd promised to never follow in his father's footsteps, and his father had promised to give up his lifelong profession.

But the promise hadn't done his father much good. Raphael Wilder had been falsely accused and convicted, and he'd died shortly after in prison.

So why should he bother to keep his promise? That was the question he'd been asking himself as he'd lunged, dribbled and shot basket after basket. And all the time she'd watched him. When he'd finally wheeled to confront her, it had been her eyes that had captured him.

He'd seen admiration and hero worship in them. Those had been balm to the raw, angry feelings of a thirteen-year-old who'd been newly orphaned.

So he'd taught her what he'd known about the game, and no teacher could have dreamed of a more responsive student.

The memory blurred for a moment. That wasn't what he should be thinking about. There was something else. Something important. Urgent. When he reached for it, pain pierced like a fiery arrow.

Curls.

This time when the image surfaced, it wasn't the child who had enchanted him, saved him when he was thirteen, but the woman who had gripped his hand and said that everything would be all right.

And it would be. He let out the breath he'd been holding and slipped under again.

To PREVENT HER TEETH from chattering, Nicola clamped them together as she dragged the last choir robes out of the closet and added them to the pile at the injured man's feet. Thank heavens there'd been a generous supply. And they were heavy.

In spite of her efforts to keep her mind on the task at hand, she couldn't prevent herself from thinking about her reaction to the man. At twenty-six, she was no stranger to desire or lust. She'd had her moments and thoroughly enjoyed them. But those feelings had never flared quite so quickly or intensely before.

And she didn't seem to have any control over them. Each time she'd added to the pile of robes, she hadn't been able to prevent herself from looking at him. And each time she did, she felt that catch of her breath, that flare of heat.

There was no logic to it. There hadn't been from the beginning.

He was a stranger. But her heart was pounding. And in spite of her determination, her mind kept spinning back to those moments in her office and just minutes ago when he'd looked into her eyes and her thoughts had clicked off just as completely as if someone had thrown a switch.

Dropping the last robe on the pile, she drew in a deep breath. *Mental list time again.* She knelt down to check her patient. His pulse was steady, the bleeding on his forehead had stopped, but she knew he had to be very cold. She certainly was. Even with the window shut, the room felt like a deep freeze. Her feet had gone numb and she'd begun to shiver.

She had to get him out of the clothes that had been drenched by the vase of water. The Paul Bunyan shirt was easy enough. Placing his arms over his head, she tugged on the sleeves. Once they were off, she finessed the rest of the shirt from under him.

His T-shirt presented more of a problem, but it had to go. In the flickering light, she could see the wet stain covered his shoulders and ran in streaks nearly to his waist. She began by tugging the material free from the waistband of his jeans. But the moment the backs of her fingers brushed against his bare skin, she knew she was in trouble, and it deepened steadily as she eased the shirt up, uncovering the narrow waist, the broad chest.

Keep your eyes on the shirt. On his face. But not on his mouth. That was a definite danger zone.

By the time she'd pushed the T-shirt up to his armpits, Nicola was aware of two things. She had some control over her eyes, but none over what she was feeling as her fingers brushed against that smooth skin stretched taut over rock-hard muscles. The little flame of lust this man had ignited in her was being fanned brighter and stronger with each contact.

She kept her eyes steady on his face, on the dark slash of brows, the shadow of a beard on that strong angled chin as she moved behind him. But her mind wandered, wondered. So far the touching had been purely clinical. Almost. And one-sided. Definitely. Still, her throat had gone dry and her pulse was racing. What would happen if she ran her hands over him with the intent of arousing him, pleasuring him? And what if he touched her back?

Whoa.

Just thinking about it stopped her teeth from chattering and made her heart pound so loudly that she was amazed the noise didn't wake him up. She carefully maneuvered the T-shirt off one arm, then the other before she eased it carefully around the wound on his forehead.

Then her gaze slid to where it had wanted to be from the beginning. She sat back on her heels and simply stared, letting her eyes feast on what her hands had already gotten more than a hint of. The muscles in his shoulders and upper arms were well-defined; his chest was broad with a triangle of thick black hair that tapered down over equally defined abs. The man was built like a Greek god. She could imagine him in bronze or sculpted in marble.

She shivered then and shook her head. She had to get a grip. He wasn't a god. He was a man who might be in shock, who was in danger of slipping into hypothermia.

Moving quickly, she grabbed one of the robes, opened it up and tucked it along the length of him from shoulders to boots on one side. Then she did the same on the other side. A part of him would still be lying on the cold marble, but there was no way she was going to be able to roll him over.

The man was so tall she had to use two of the shorter robes to fully cover him. After she'd arranged them, she leaned down and patted his cheek again.

"It's going to be all right," she said.

His lashes fluttered. "C...c...old."

"I know. You'll be warm soon. I promise."

How soon? That was the crucial question. There were only two robes left. She'd had some idea of using them for herself.

She glanced at her coat. It was damp on the outside. And she was going to have to get out of her wet slacks and boots.

And then what?

Nicola very carefully avoided looking at the man. Because the answer was obvious. And it had been there lurking in the back of her mind ever since she'd started undressing him.

She was an FBI agent. She'd been trained in survival tactics, and the quickest, most efficient way to keep both of them warm—for the time being—was to share everything. Including body heat.

And the only reason she was stalling was because of the effect this man—this complete stranger—had on her senses. Annoyed—no, angry at herself, Nicola arranged the last two robes. They were both adults. And she was the only fully conscious one. What was her problem?

She tugged off her boots. If he tried anything, she could

handle herself. Shrugging out of her holster, she placed it next to her gun and the flashlight.

But what if you *try something?*

"Not happening," Nicola muttered as she wiggled out of her wet trousers. A little fantasizing, a little lust. She could handle it.

But she didn't look at him as she joined him beneath the pile of robes.

Every muscle in her body tensed when his arm snaked around her and pulled her close. Suddenly she was wrapped around him as intimately as a lover—her thigh across his, her head nestled into the crook of his shoulder. She might have objected if she hadn't felt a blast of warmth at each and every contact point.

Or if he'd moved another muscle.

But he didn't.

She waited, counting the seconds...five...ten...fifteen... twenty.

But the only thing that moved was the rise and fall of his chest beneath her palm. Still, she kept her eyes open, her mind alert as the seconds stretched into minutes.

But he lay there, still as a stone. And all the while the warmth spread, slowly, deliciously until she was certain she could feel it penetrate her muscles and even her bones. The instant she could feel her toes again and wiggle them, she considered moving. It would be the prudent thing to do.

And she'd always figured herself for a practical kind of woman.

He was warm now. She could feel the heat of his skin beneath her palm and along her stomach where her jacket had pulled open. It was probably safe to move away. It was probably safer to move away.

The yawn took her by surprise. Even more surprising

was the realization that at some point she'd relaxed fully against him. And she didn't want to move.

Not the most practical decision. She'd reconsider it in a minute. Just one more minute…

4

GABE SURFACED QUICKLY this time and began to orient himself. There was still pain thrumming at the back of his head and near his temple.

The fight.

The details were there, but he pushed them away for now, along with the pain. Both were secondary.

Primary was the flood of sensations storming through his system because of the woman. He was surrounded by them, trapped by them. The pressure of each one of the fingers splayed across his chest might have been a brand. The leg she'd thrown across him imprisoned his thighs and ignited an almost uncontrollable fire in his loins. His whole body was aroused, throbbing.

Who?

Opening his eyes, he shifted slowly until their positions were reversed. Her head lay in the crook of his arm, and it was his leg that held her prisoner now. Even as her eyelashes fluttered and then stilled, recognition streamed through him.

Nicola Guthrie.

What the hell was she doing here? He gave his head a shake, hoping to clear the fog. Pain stabbed. He shut his eyes against it and gritted his teeth as he willed details into place.

He remembered Father Mike's phone call about the note, the long drive through the storm. He'd arrived at the church, hoping to surprise the thief. Instead, he'd been the one surprised. He recalled the open window that had lured him into the choir room and the blow to his head. But it hadn't taken him out. He'd managed that on his own. The last thing he could dredge up was his feet flying out from beneath him. That's when the fireworks had exploded in his brain.

Moving more carefully this time, he glanced around the room. A flashlight and candles provided the only illumination. That and the howling of the wind outside told him that the storm hadn't let up. He should get up and check on the statue. But he was confident that his new alarm system had held, and his prayers to St. Francis had worked.

This time.

He glanced back down at Nicola. None of what he remembered explained why FBI special agent Nicola Guthrie was here, lying beneath him on the floor of the choir room.

Except…

He frowned as the image slipped into focus—her face filling his vision, her voice telling him everything would be all right. Assuring him that both statues were still here. He thought he'd been dreaming. Just as he'd dreamed of her too often in the past three months.

Because he'd known from the first instant he'd seen her in the FBI office that Nicola Guthrie spelled trouble for him with capital letters. When she'd met his eyes in that brief instant of contact, he'd felt everything else slip away until there'd only been her. The wanting had started that instant, and he hadn't been able to shake free of it.

So he'd avoided her like the plague for nearly three months. Although he'd consulted on the case, he'd never once set foot in the FBI office. Nick Guthrie was a good friend, one he owed. One he intended to keep. And the flare of hot, primitive desire he'd felt in that one meeting of glances with Nicola was the last thing he wanted to feel for a friend's daughter. Getting involved with her meant complications, and where women were concerned, he liked to keep his relationships simple. He'd even managed to avoid her during the past few weeks when she'd started tailing him during the evening hours. He had a pretty good idea why. Nick Guthrie might be convinced that he'd had nothing to do with the robberies. But it was a more than good bet that someone at G. W. Securities was up to his or her neck in them. So Guthrie had assigned Nicola to follow him—just to cover all his bases.

Gabe was fine with that. What he wasn't fine with was that having her on his tail had only increased the number of times she'd slipped into his thoughts each day—especially when he'd been working here at the church on the security for the statue.

He couldn't keep her out of his mind. That scared him. It ticked him off. It also fascinated him. No one, nothing had ever pulled at him the way she did.

And she was doing it again now. Without even trying. She was asleep, totally unaware of him. Like Sleeping Beauty, blissfully ignorant of the effect she was having on him. He should get up, move. But he couldn't seem to make his body obey.

Baffled, he studied her in the dim light, taking in the creamy porcelain skin, the sprinkling of freckles. Before he could prevent himself he brushed a strand of hair off of her cheek and behind her ear. At that simple contact of skin against skin, desire shot through him, a rusty claw in his gut.

He'd spent nearly three months being prudent and safe. Perhaps it was time to try a different tack.

One taste. That's what he told himself as he leaned closer and began to tease her lips apart with his. One taste. He rubbed his mouth softly over hers, then unable to stop himself, he sank in.

Her lips were soft. He'd imagined they would be. And warm. He'd expected that also. But when he finally slipped his tongue between them, he found a surprising mix of flavors. Cool and hot, sweet and pungent. Each flavor drew him, tempted him to taste and taste again.

She began to tremble. That, more than her flavors, undermined his resolve and he plunged in to take the kiss deeper.

IT WAS LIKE WAKING UP in the heart of a firestorm. One minute she'd been fast asleep, and the next, every nerve in her body was alive, burning, yearning. Before she could think, she wrapped her arms and legs around him and held on.

His mouth was so hot and nearly savage. The press of his body against hers vibrated through her right down to her bones. And the feelings he aroused in her were so vivid. So new. Desire had never been this sharp. Hunger had never gone this deep. Need had never been this demanding.

In some far corner of her brain where rationality hadn't been burned to cinders, she heard a voice telling her she had to think. The practical Nicola. But how could she pay any heed when her pulse was pounding in her head and his taste, ripe and rich, was pouring through her like a drug?

She wanted more. She had to have more. When he slipped a hand beneath her jacket and slid it up her bare skin to cover her breast, she arched, determined to get even closer to that hard, rangy body. Oh, yes, she had to have more. A sound, something primitive, clawed its way out of her throat.

As if in answer, he used his teeth, scraping them along her bottom lip before he moved his mouth to her neck. With sensations hammering through her system, she heard the practical voice again. This couldn't be right, shouldn't be right. But every nerve in her body tingled with the conviction blossoming inside of her that it was. Exactly right.

Stop. The word had become a chant in his head, but Gabe's body ignored the order. She was all wild flavors and silken textures, and she was driving him crazy. Wherever he touched or tasted, she responded with a huge unreserved pleasure that fascinated him. Captured him.

He'd thought about what it would be like ever since that first meeting of eyes. But any fantasies he'd entertained fell far short of reality. He hadn't wanted her to stir up this kind of primitive need. But hadn't he known she would? He slid his hands down to her hips, and when she arched up and tightened her legs around him, the only thing that kept him from taking what he was craving was that he was still wearing his jeans. His fingers were struggling with the snap when he recalled how he'd started this, kissing her when she was still asleep. He'd taken her this far without an invitation. Stealing a kiss without asking was one thing, but he wanted more...

He drew his head up then and brought her face into focus. She was awake now. He could see himself in those chocolate-colored eyes. She held him just as surely there as she did with her arms and legs. A warning bell sounded, but it was distant.

"You stopped," she said.

Her voice might have been a throaty murmur, but there was a note of accusation in the tone.

"Paused," he corrected. "And I won't stop if I kiss you again," he stated. "I wanted to make sure you were on board with that."

For a moment she said nothing. But she didn't move.

Neither did he.

In his mind, he might intend to play the gentleman, but his body hadn't gotten the memo. He was very much aware that they were pressed closely together, center to center, heat to heat, with nothing more than denim and her panties separating them. His body throbbed at every point a pulse could beat.

He rocked into her, saw the heat flare in her eyes, felt the shudder move through her body. One thread of whatever control he had left snapped.

"It would be a mistake." Her voice was barely a whisper.

"We're on the same page there." It would be a huge mistake. Hadn't he given himself that lecture countless times? But he'd also known that this moment was coming, that as hard as he might try, he wouldn't be able to prevent it from happening.

He ran his mouth along her jaw, then nipped at her chin. "What do you say?"

Say? She wasn't at all sure that she could form a word. But even as she desperately reached for one, she wrapped her arms and legs more tightly around him. The heat, the glorious blast of it was so intense, she felt as if she'd been caught in a sudden back draft of flames. There was pleasure pulsing through her in an endless stream until it was all she could feel. He was all she could feel.

And he felt so right. She was very aware of the hardness of the floor beneath her. His body was even harder and so hot that she wanted nothing more than to melt into him. She caught herself before she arched against him again. If she did, she might climax. She could feel it almost within reach.

"I should think..."

Had she said the words aloud? She must have because he drew back enough to meet her eyes, and there was a question in his. There was also a glint of something dark and reckless that ignited that familiar tingle deep within her. Her practical side might want to worry about mistakes and consequences, but something much closer to the bone ruled. Some mistakes were worth making.

"I want you so much," she said.

He kissed her then, and she felt that wonderful heat began to build inside of her again. She knew what happened when you played with fire. But she wanted the flash point. And she wanted it now. She tightened her legs around him and arched again.

He immediately gripped her hips and stilled her movements. Then he lifted his head.

She tried to move and couldn't. "You said the next time you kissed me you wouldn't stop."

"Protection." His voice was hoarse. "I don't—"

"We're good." She dragged his mouth back to hers and nipped his bottom lip.

"We're about to get even better," he promised. "But first, we have to get rid of the clothes."

"Oh...right." But she kept her mouth on his the whole time his hands slid between them to push down his jeans. Her clothes weren't an issue. He pushed the thin lace of her panties aside and slid a finger into her. "Now, come for me."

He gave her no choice. The climax that had been threatening erupted through her in wave after wave, each one sharper than the last. Helpless, she gave herself over to it and to the man who was giving it to her.

Her body was still quaking from the last ripple when he drew his finger out and pressed the head of his penis against the slick heat of her core. He wanted to go slowly, but her response, her surrender, were so much more than he'd imagined. How much further could she take him? Raising his head, he said, "Look at me."

She opened her eyes, and he watched them go wide and blurry as he thrust into her in one stroke. She was hotter and tighter than he'd expected. The feel of her muscles trembling and tugging urged him to go deeper. Hooking his arms around her legs, he lifted them so that he could push even more fully into her.

Her eyes went dark, then blind with pleasure. And for a moment he was sure his own did the same. He couldn't think of anything but the mating of their bodies. He couldn't even move. All he could do was sink farther and farther into her. The thought of withdrawing even a little, even to push into her again—he couldn't do it. This was where he wanted to stay. Where he belonged.

But as she continued to contract around him, the pulse of his own release tore through him. He tried to hold back, to hold her, to hold them both where they were right now. But as another climax radiated through her in little convulsions, his own pleasure overcame him, consuming him and finally overpowering him completely.

5

REALITY TRICKLED IN slowly. Nicola heard the sound of breathing, slightly ragged, but she couldn't tell if it was him or her. She could smell the faint tang of incense, and him—soap and water and something that was very male. She was still wrapped around him.

And he was still inside of her.

Without any hesitation, she grasped him, let go, then grasped him again.

"Ready?" He whispered the question in her ear even as she felt him grow harder inside of her.

"Mmm."

He gripped her hips and eased her into a rhythm.

Pleasure shot through her, but she managed to raise her head, just enough to meet his eyes. "I'm not…not usually. I don't understand…. It's you."

"Or you," he countered as his fingers dug into her hips and he abruptly increased the speed of his thrusts.

Then it didn't matter, not with his heart pounding against hers, beat to beat. Not with pleasure pummeling through her again and again with each thrust. She couldn't think, didn't want to. Not while she could take this wild ride to that place where there were only the two of them and only the intense pleasure that they could bring each other.

He cried out first as he drove into her one last time and the world around them shattered.

GABE WOKE TO FIND Nicola still sprawled on top of him. The steady sound of her breath going in and out signaled that she was asleep. And he could no longer hear the sound of the wind outside. In its place, he caught the closer clank of a radiator heating up, so the power and the furnace were back on.

Opening his eyes, he lay perfectly still, taking a moment to orient himself. The light overhead was also on. He lifted his arm to glance at his watch. After midnight. So roughly three hours had passed since he'd arrived at the church. When he turned his head, pain poked at his forehead, but it was manageable. The back of his head throbbed a bit, but his memory of what had happened was crystal clear. He hadn't caught the thief.

Instead, he'd caught Nicola Guthrie. Ready or not. He shifted his gaze to the top of her head. Her scent reminded him of spring flowers. And she felt right lying on top of him. The fact that he didn't want to move might have worried him, but his more immediate concern was that he was still inside of her. So there was a definite part of him that did want to move.

Just thinking about what it would feel like had him growing harder. It wasn't that he didn't want to make love to her again. He did. But he wanted to do it under different circumstances. A bed might be nice. Something with a little more room, a little more give than a cold, hard marble floor.

And wasn't this just the trouble he'd intended to avoid? Having her just this once wasn't going to do it for him.

He'd suspected that from the first time he'd looked at her through that glass wall.

Now there would be complications. Big ones. And he already had a lot on his plate.

Gripping her hips, he lifted her, then hoping not to wake her, he shifted slowly so that they were lying side by side. Her head was still tucked into his shoulder.

Progress. But not enough, especially when he wanted nothing more than to stay right where he was. This time it wasn't desire pulling at him, but a warmth that was even more seductive. Though he couldn't explain it, holding her close felt right. Against all logic and in spite of everything he'd done to try and prevent this from happening, it had.

Nicola had nearly protested when he'd shifted her. Instead, she continued to play possum for a few more minutes. It wasn't that she wanted him to make love to her again. Although if he made a move, she was pretty sure she would respond. She didn't seem to have any way to stop herself.

And this just wasn't like her. She'd never been so impulsive, so reckless with a man before. She had to break contact with him completely and get back to being FBI special agent Nicola Guthrie. She just needed another second to think of what she was supposed to do next.

What should she say? How could she explain what had happened, what she'd done, when she didn't understand it herself?

She'd been on duty. She'd been pursuing a thief who'd gotten away, and the man she'd just made love to…twice… might know something important that would solve the case.

Then there was her father. She had to find a way to contact him and let him know that Gabe Wilder had nearly stolen the statue of St. Francis. In short, she had a job to do, and snuggling under the covers with a perfect stranger, no matter how tempting it might be, could not be on the top of her to-do list. But how to get him off of it was the problem.

Back to business, Nicola. Move.

But it was the stranger who began to inch away.

Drawing in a deep breath, she opened her eyes and fastened them on his. She felt the impact of his gaze right down to her toes.

"You're awake," he said.

"I have been for a while," she confessed. "I was just trying to figure out what to say to you." She still didn't have a clue. And looking into his eyes wasn't helping. Dragging her gaze away, she fastened it on the cut on his forehead. "Your head. Are you all right?"

Guilt overcame her. She'd forgotten all about his injuries when she'd awakened the first time. The man had been unconscious and bleeding when she'd found him.

"I could use half a bottle of aspirin."

"I'm sorry. I'm so sorry."

His brows snapped together. "For what?"

"For…for…jumping you when you had clearly sustained head injuries. I checked your eyes to see if they were dilated—but I'm not a doctor."

"Are they dilated now?"

She studied them for a minute. "No." She raised her index finger in front of his face. "When I move it to the left and right, follow it with your eyes."

He did. "What's my prognosis?"

"Your eyes seem fine. But all of my medical knowledge comes from a mandatory first aid course I took. Or TV. You should definitely go to an emergency room." She started to move away, but he gripped her shoulders and held her in place. "For the record, the jumping was mutual. And I'm the one who took the initial step."

"You'd been unconscious. I should never have crawled under the covers with you… And you gave me a chance to stop things. I didn't."

And she wasn't moving away right now. In fact, if he gave her the least little bit of encouragement… No. She was going to move. Away. And she would have if he hadn't chosen that particular moment to smile. Her bones began to melt.

"Are you seriously trying to argue that you took advantage of me, Curls? I assure you that you didn't."

"Curls?" She blinked, then stared at him as fragmented images filled her mind the way they might have swirled into place in a kaleidoscope. She gave her head a shake. In denial? But the images didn't fade. She was back at the St. Francis Center playing basketball on the small streetside court. With Gabe Wilder.

He took a strand of her hair and tucked it behind her ear. "I miss your curls. Remember when I used to tug on them?"

The widening of his smile transformed the ripples of recognition that had been lapping at the edge of her mind into a full-blown wave. And she did remember. He'd often tugged her hair to push her into making a more aggressive play. She'd hated it. And he'd always called her Curls. She'd hated that, too.

"Gabe." She stared at him, hoping against hope that she was wrong. "You're Gabe Wilder."

"Guilty."

She closed her eyes. Perhaps when she opened them, she would find that it had all been a dream. But her practical side was reasserting itself with a vengeance, and she definitely hadn't dreamed what had happened. No way. Dreams never rocked your world. That was a job for reality.

So she'd deal. She would find a way to solve the problem. But when she opened her eyes, the only thing she wanted to deal with was right there in front of her. And she didn't want to move except to pull him closer and to feel his mouth on hers again.

"No. No. No."

That wasn't happening. And there was only one person she could blame for the fact that it ever had. Well, maybe two. When a tiny flicker of anger sprang to life, she finally found the strength to place her hands on his shoulders and push hard. Then she wiggled out from beneath the pile of robes.

The marble floor beneath her butt might just as well have been a block of ice. Her skimpy lace panties provided no protection. She felt around on the floor for her slacks.

"I can assure you that I am Gabe Wilder. I can even show you some I.D."

"No, you can't. I checked for your wallet before and it was gone." Then she made the big mistake of looking at him. He'd risen and was in the process of pulling his jeans into place. But before they got there, she got a good look at those long legs, the narrow hips and waist, and his... Her mouth went dry.

He checked his pockets, then frowned. "I'm missing my car keys, too."

"That's not all. The other guy took your car, too. Black SUV." She rattled off the license plate.

"He stole my car?"

"I saw him drive away in it. That's why I assumed *you* were not Gabe Wilder."

"Interesting."

"Interesting? It's more than that," she managed to say as

her brain cells began to click on again. "This whole thing is totally unfair. If I had known who you were, I never should have…we never should have…"

"Spilled milk, don't you think?"

"Think? That's just it. I wasn't thinking. If I'd known you were Gabe Wilder, I never would have…" She waved a hand. "Never. He…you were my prime suspect. I was sure that you were connected to the thefts. You had to be. I always get this feeling when I'm right about something."

"What things?"

"Applying to the FBI for a job, coming back here to Denver to work for my dad." Playing basketball with you when I was ten. But she didn't blurt that part out. "I'm not usually wrong."

When he walked over to her and squatted down so that he could meet her eyes, she stifled the urge to wiggle away. Instead, she lifted her chin and locked her eyes on his. She was going to figure out a way to handle him.

"You didn't recognize me."

"No." Since he was frowning, she frowned right back at him. "How was I supposed to? I haven't seen you since we were kids."

"Except for that one time when I visited your father. I saw you through the glass wall of your office. I wanted you that day. And you wanted me, too."

She swallowed hard, but she kept her eyes steady on his. "It's been fifteen years and you weren't wearing a name tag."

"Who did you think I was?"

Nicola felt the flame of anger inside of her grow. She hadn't been thinking then either. She'd just been feeling. "I assumed you were a client, someone who had business with the FBI."

He was interrogating her. And her butt was growing number by the second. Not to mention her toes.

"Not then. Who did you think I was when you crawled in with me?"

"Do you mind?" She would have gotten to her feet if she could have managed it without touching him. "I'm freezing here. I'd like to get dressed."

"Sorry." He picked up her slacks. "These are soaked from the knees down." After draping them on a nearby radiator, he took her hands and pulled her to her feet. Then turning, he picked up two robes and handed her one. "I'm sure Father Mike won't mind if we borrow these."

Nicola said nothing as she slipped into it. The material pooled around her feet. Gabe's robe, on the other hand, fell just below his knees.

"Your boots and socks are soaked, too," he said as he placed them on the radiator next to his shirt.

Then he turned to her. "Ready?"

"For what?"

Before she even had time to protest, he scooped her up in his arms and strode out toward the altar. "I want to check on the statues. Don't you?"

"Yes." Of course she did. That was what she should be thinking about, not… Then she was sitting in a front pew, her legs stretched out in front of her, and he was tucking the robe around her feet.

"Stay here. The thief didn't steal my cell. I'm going to see if it works."

"I couldn't get a signal earlier."

He tossed a grin over his shoulder as he climbed the steps to the side altar. "You've got to know where to stand to pick it up. When I was installing the alarm, I learned the only place to get a signal in the place is right here by

St. Francis. I'll update your father. He can put an APB out on my car."

Nicola frowned as she watched him push in numbers. "Nick, it's Gabe."

There was a short pause, and then he began to fill her father in on what had happened. Clearly, Gabe wasn't having any trouble prioritizing what they should be focusing on. *He* was not only reporting to her father—something she should be doing, but he was trying to dry out their clothes and making arrangements for them to be picked up.

While her mind was still stuck on…him and what she was going to do. What she should do and what she wanted to do were miles apart.

Spilled milk. You cleaned it up and moved on. That was clearly his attitude. And perhaps she should take her cue from him. What was done couldn't be undone. Just forgetting about it and moving on was the practical solution. Except she wasn't going to be able to forget what had happened. What they'd done. She drew in a deep breath, gave her head a mental shake. She had to get her focus back on stopping the robberies, catching the thief.

"The road crews are out, but travel is not recommended." Gabe sat down in the pew and stretched one arm along the back. She felt the heat of it instantly.

"Your father is sending a helicopter for us. Its ETA is approximately forty-five minutes from now. So we have some time to kill."

Her eyes collided with his, and for a moment her brain cells shut down again. Worse, she didn't want to put any effort into resuscitating them. Everything inside of her yearned for him.

And he felt it, too. She could see that telltale gleam in his eyes and read the question as clearly as if he'd spoken it aloud.

Ready?

They weren't even touching, yet she was definitely ready. Ready to go anywhere he would take her. Ready to take that glorious leap into the world of sensation only he'd shown her.

But she shouldn't. They couldn't. As much as she wished she could.

Focus, Nicola told herself. Time to summon up a mental list that didn't start off with jumping back under the covers with Gabe Wilder.

It didn't help her concentration at all when he smiled at her and the effect sizzled right down to her toes.

She drew in a breath she wasn't even aware that she needed. "There's a thief out there that we have to catch." She said the words aloud for herself as much as Gabe. "I have a lot of questions. For starters, what are you doing here?"

"I'll be happy to answer that as soon as you answer two questions for me."

"Two?" She narrowed her eyes on his.

"I've already asked one of them. And then I'll answer two for you. Deal?"

Nicola studied him and thought of the Gabe she'd known when she was ten. He'd been a tease then, too, often tormenting her to get her to push just a little harder on the court. "What's your first question?"

"The curls." He lifted a strand of her hair and rubbed it between his fingers. "I really miss them."

"All you ever did was pull them."

"It made you angry and you played better ball."

Her brows shot up. "That's your excuse?"

He grinned. "And I'm sticking to it."

She saw the gleam in his eyes again, the one that had

fascinated her when she was ten. And the intervening years had only increased its effect.

He tugged on the strand of hair he'd been holding. "Where have they gone?"

"That's your first question?"

"Uh-huh."

The only thing that kept her from rolling her eyes was the fact that the quickest way she was going to get the answers to her questions was to humor him. "I use a flattening iron."

"Pity." Then the smile faded from his eyes. "Who did you think I was when you made love to me?"

That was the biggy, Nicola thought. And it was one she wanted answers to, also. But she was pretty sure she wasn't going to like them. "A stranger." Not good. "An injured man." Even worse. "I don't understand it. You were right. I wanted you that day when I saw you in the office. I haven't been able to stop wanting you. I didn't know you, and you were injured."

When he opened his mouth, she held up a hand to stop him. "And for the record, I don't make a habit of crawling under the covers with every hunky-looking stranger I meet. The problem was I wasn't thinking."

That was true enough. But it wasn't everything. And she needed to figure it out. If she could just get the right perspective, she could handle it. "You were lying on the floor and I had to bring you back to consciousness. The moment you opened your eyes, I recognized that you were the man in the office that day, and I wanted you. Just like that. I simply can't explain it."

"Yeah," Gabe said. "I think we're in the same boat, Curls."

For a moment neither of them spoke. She saw something flicker in his eyes and it triggered that tingling feeling inside of her. The one she'd felt when they'd been making love. That it was…just right.

She hurried on. "It never occurred to me that you were Gabe Wilder. Not then, and certainly not tonight. I'd just chased Gabe Wilder out of here. I'd even taken a shot at him, and he drove away in your SUV."

"Did you manage to hit the thief?" Gabe asked.

She shook her head. "I don't think so. I certainly didn't slow him down any."

"Wait here." She watched him rise and walk down the side aisle, his eyes on the floor. He was nearly at the end when he stopped and crouched down. "Blood. Your aim was on target, Curls."

Nicola felt her stomach knot, and she wasn't relieved at all by the grim expression on Gabe's face when he rejoined her in the pew. "Our thief got more than he bargained for this time."

When she said nothing, he reached out and covered her hand with his. "First time you've shot someone?"

"Yeah." As he linked his fingers with hers, she felt the knot in her stomach loosen.

"Why don't you take me through it? Everything that happened from the time you arrived."

She did. By the time she'd finished her narrative, Gabe knew three things. First, she had courage. But he'd already seen that when she was ten years old. Looking back, he could see that it had taken a good deal of it to accept his invitation to play basketball that day. Nearly as much as it had taken her to race up the aisle when she'd heard the sounds of a fight.

She was definitely a risk taker. And she had an excellent eye for detail. She'd spotted an abandoned car in the ditch that he'd missed and she'd seen the second statue. He didn't imagine there was much that escaped her notice.

Maybe she was just what he needed—fresh eyes on the robberies.

"That takes us right up until I crawled under the covers with you," Nicola wound up. "And none of what happened there pertains to the case."

"Indirectly, it does, Curls. I think by crawling in with me, you just may have saved my life."

She narrowed her eyes on him. "Don't get overly dramatic. In spite of your injuries, you don't seem much the worse for wear."

The dryness of her tone had him smiling. "Who knows how long it would have taken for someone to have found me? Hypothermia can be life-threatening. I owe you."

"For doing my job."

He raised her hand and skimmed his mouth over her fingers.

Just that brief contact had sensation flooding her system. "Don't," she managed to say. "We need to concentrate on the case. On catching the thief."

He had to agree with her on that one. But the pulse beating at her throat, the breathiness in her voice had him wanting badly to multitask. Reluctantly, he released her hand. "I still owe you."

Nicola glanced back up at the statues. "At least the thief didn't get St. Francis."

Gabe followed her gaze. "No chance of that this time. I designed a new alarm system, a prototype that isn't even in production yet. No one at G. W. has seen it. I called in a favor from a friend at the *Denver Post* and she wrote that feature article on the statue of St. Francis in last Sunday's paper. I was hoping it might lure the thief out here."

Nicola shifted her gaze to Gabe. "You set the statue up as bait? All of the other art pieces the thief has taken have been paintings. How did you know he'd come after it?"

"It was Father Mike's idea. He thought it might be helpful to involve the statue. Whoever is behind these robberies seems to have an affinity for G. W. Securities' systems. I was also depending on the statue's spreading reputation for granting answers to prayers. There are a lot of eccentric collectors out there who would pay a lot for that." He shrugged. "I also said a prayer that the trap would work."

"St. Francis evidently answered it this time."

"Except the thief came early and got away."

For the first time, she heard a hint of emotion in his voice. And she thought of the anger and frustration he must be feeling. He'd had his hands on the thief. She turned and met his eyes. "He couldn't have been happy when he didn't get the statue."

"That's probably why my wallet, keys and car are missing—to let me know that I was helpless to stop it. I think that's partly what the robberies are about—to let me know that G. W. Securities can't prevent them. At least we haven't until today."

He rose from the pew and paced a few steps away. "I've told your father that whatever is going on here, it's connected to me personally somehow. It's not just a coincidence that the thief uses my father's M.O."

"I've told him the same thing," Nicola said. "But I also suggested strongly the possibility that you were behind the thefts. He wasn't open to that."

"Don't worry. He'll arrest me if he can get enough evidence. That's the kind of man he is." He studied her for a moment. "Did he ask you to tail me?"

"No—how did you know I was tailing me?"

"Curls, my business is providing security. I spotted you the first day. I figured your father had assigned you just as a precaution."

"Ever since he had me transferred to his office, all he's

asked me to do is research. I wouldn't be here now if Father Mike had come to the office a half hour earlier. And when I made it up here and found your car parked outside the church, I was so sure you had to be the thief."

"Can't blame you." Gabe took a seat next to her again. "And now?"

She tilted her head and studied him for a moment. A tall man, broad shouldered, wearing a robe that didn't fit. Everything inside of her yearned for him.

Not good. "I'm not sure I can be objective anymore."

He smiled at her, then ran a finger down her cheek. "I'm that good, huh?"

Nicola raised an eyebrow, firmly ignoring the killer smile as well as the ribbon of heat that unwound through her veins until it curled her toes. "Evidently, *we're* that good. Your theory is that it was a mutual jumping, remember?"

"Yes, I do remember, Curls. Every detail. Want to talk about it?"

"No." She didn't even want to think about it. Though she would. She was sure of it. Later. "You said it was spilled milk. I agree. And I think we have more important things to discuss. Your turn to answer my questions. What are you doing here?"

He nodded in the direction of the statue. "I got a call from Father Mike the instant he received the note. I told him to go report to your father. And just to put it on the record, I'm not behind the thefts."

"Do you have any idea who is?"

The easy smile faded and his eyes turned cold. "The person or persons behind the thefts are either working for me or getting information from someone inside G. W. Securities. Or they're working in your office. That's why I didn't share any information on the prototype, not even with your dad. And one of the people involved is also intimately familiar with my father's methods."

"You think there's more than one person involved?"

"There has to be. There aren't a lot of thieves as multi-talented as my father was. He was a regular Houdini when it came to locks or safes, but he might have been even better at creating forgeries."

"You've examined the ones these thieves have left behind?"

He nodded. "They're excellent. And they match up in quality to the ones my dad did himself. Plus, he always signed his work with R.W. That detail isn't very well-known." He glanced toward the altar. "Let's see if this one is signed."

Nicola stayed right where she was as Gabe retrieved the statue she'd placed there earlier. There'd been both admiration and love in his tone when he'd spoken of his father. Her mind flashed back to the boy she'd first seen on that basketball court. He'd been orphaned, left alone, at thirteen. Within a very short time he'd lost two people he'd clearly loved. But he'd worked past that. And now fifteen years later, someone was digging up all those memories.

Even worse, it wouldn't be long before the press got hold of the details that would rake up Raphael Wilder's career and his connection to Gabe. The same details that had caused her to point the finger at Gabe Wilder as the prime suspect.

Gabe settled himself once more in the pew. "You won't be able to see it clearly in this light." He took her hand and rubbed her fingers along the base of the statue.

"Can you feel the swirl in the R and the W?"

What Nicola felt was a tingle, but she traced her fingers across the base again to make sure before she met Gabe's eyes.

"What is it?"

"I feel the W all right. But the other letter isn't an R. It feels more like a G."

Gabe immediately turned the statue over and examined it in the light. First he examined the base, running his fingers across the letters just as she had. Then he ran his hands carefully over every inch of the entire statue.

"Is the thief signing your initials now?"

Gabe met her eyes. "No. I signed this statue myself. Years ago."

6

"YOU SCULPTED THIS STATUE?"

Gabe shook his head. "No. The summer after my mother died, my father worked on it and some other pieces in her art studio. It was an old gardener's cottage she'd renovated and used for her own painting. I would sit on a stool and watch him. On this piece, he tried to teach me how to use the tools, and after I'd hacked up the marble, he'd smooth over my mistakes. I didn't inherit either his artistic talent or my mother's."

As the memories slipped into his mind, so did the mix of emotions that always accompanied those memories of his father. Gabe set the statue down in front of him and leaned back in the pew. "We finished the statue and I signed it just a few weeks before he was arrested and taken away."

And why in hell had he brought that up? He didn't talk about his father's arrest. It was a part of his life that he preferred to never revisit.

It was only as Nicola covered one of his hands that he realized he'd fisted his. When she said nothing, he spoke again. "He and I didn't have much time together. My parents met in Paris where she was studying painting, and it was love at first sight. But aside from their shared talent in painting, they couldn't have been more different. He was from the streets, and she came from wealth. Plus, he was already well on his way to becoming one of the most successful art thieves in Europe. After I was born, she brought me back here to Denver to raise me. She wanted me to have a normal upbringing, a quiet life, and he simply couldn't settle down. Stealing things, creating the forgeries to leave as replacements, running the cons—it was all a wonderful game to him, one he couldn't give up. But they never stopped loving each other."

"One grew up, the other didn't. They sound like Peter Pan and Wendy," Nicola murmured.

"That's not a bad analogy. I think they were very happy with the compromise they'd worked out. She'd inherited an estate and a small fortune from her parents, so she raised me here while he traveled the world. Until I was twelve, my father was someone I only saw on holidays. He never missed one. Then my mother became ill with cancer, and he came home to stay. He brought his friend Bennett Carter with him. When my mom became bedridden, Uncle Ben took over the running of the household and supervised the care my mother needed." Gabe's lips curved. "According to my dad, Uncle Ben used to work for one branch of Britain's Royals, and he was the best treasure Raphael Wilder ever nipped."

"Your father was especially talented at reproducing paintings, wasn't he? There was no mention of sculpting in the research I did on him."

"No." He was frowning when he met her eyes. "But I remember he had pieces of marble delivered to our home."

"Do you have any idea why he might have wanted to copy the statue of St. Francis?"

Gabe's frown deepened. "No. We spent a lot of time together after Mom died. One of the places we used to go together was the St. Francis Center. My dad would talk with Father Mike in the little garden while I played basketball with my friends."

"Jonah and Nash—the ones who always interrupted our games."

Meeting her eyes, he lifted a hand to tug at a strand of her hair. "Good memory, Curls."

"Do you know what Father Mike and your father talked about?"

"I assumed they talked about my mom. Father Mike visited the house often when she was ill."

Nicola let two beats go by. "Do you think your father was planning to steal the statue?"

"No." Then Gabe sighed at the vehemence of his tone. "He promised my mother on her deathbed that he would never steal ever again. I've always believed that he kept his word."

Nicola didn't argue, and when she squeezed his hand again, he linked his fingers with hers and felt some of the turmoil of feelings inside of him settle.

"When we started working on the piece of marble together, he never mentioned that it would be a copy of St. Francis. He said that the marble knew what was inside. It was our job to discover it."

"Well, one thing I can say. I'm beginning to be happier that I shot the thief."

"Why?" Her tone surprised him; so did the spark of anger in her eyes. Releasing his hand, she rose from the pew and, grabbing fistfuls of the robe, began to pace.

"You said that these robberies are personal, and you were right. If this guy had succeeded in taking the real statue and substituting that one, you might have been arrested. The press would have had a field day. And even when you were eventually released, the reputation of G. W. Securities would have been damaged. Badly."

For a moment, he said nothing. There were too many feelings running through him. He couldn't have even named all of them. She was only giving voice to the growing certainty he'd had ever since the first robbery. But having her say the words, knowing that she believed them, filled a space inside of him that he hadn't even been aware of. "A few hours ago you were entertaining the idea I was the mastermind behind the robberies."

She whirled back to face him. "I was wrong about that. But not wrong about the fact that you hold the key. And you may be at the center of it all."

"The center?"

She moved back to the pew. "What if the thefts aren't about the art? What if they're about destroying you?"

He considered it. If she was right, that did shift the perspective a bit. Opened up new possibilities. But... "Why?"

"That's the question we should be asking."

"The art has to figure in some way."

She nodded. "Sure. We've got a good forger in partnership with someone who knows his way around systems. But why are they using your father's M.O.—except to get at you?" She sat down and took his hands in hers. "I know I'm right. That's why I was so focused on you."

For a moment, Gabe couldn't speak because he was so focused on her. The instant she'd touched him, it was just as if someone had thrown a switch. Now he felt nothing but the torrent of liquid heat she alone had the power to set off in him. And nothing else mattered. Nothing else existed but her.

It was happening to her, too. Her eyes had darkened until her irises were only a shade darker than her pupils. And he felt each one of her fingers tighten on his hand. He could hear each one of the breaths she drew in and expelled.

His gaze dropped to her mouth. Her lips were parted, waiting. All he had to do was move a few inches and he could taste her again. If he did…

For a moment, he let himself imagine stripping her out of that robe and making love to her right there. He could picture her as she would look in the flickering light of the candles. He could touch her the way he hadn't been able to before.

There was a sound outside, not unlike the noise the blizzard had made at its peak. "I think that's our ride, looking for a spot to land," Gabe said.

"Clothes," Nicola muttered.

She led the way back to the radiator in the choir room. How she'd gotten to her feet or how she managed to walk on legs she couldn't feel was a mystery she couldn't fathom. If the helicopter hadn't been landing, they would have made love again—right there.

And that was *not* what she should be thinking about. Ruthlessly, she made a mental list. First, clothes. Then the thefts.

While she pulled on damp slacks, Nicola kept trying to put the pieces together like a puzzle in her mind. The robberies, the forgeries, and the holidays and Gabe Wilder. There had to be a way to make them all fit. If she focused on that, she wouldn't be tempted to look at Gabe. But when she heard his robe drop to the floor, she wasn't able to prevent herself from stealing one quick peek. And for an instant the puzzle pieces scattered.

His back was turned to her, and for a moment, she couldn't drag her gaze away from those broad shoulders, the skin stretched smooth over well defined muscles. Her breath caught in her throat, her heart began to pound and her palms itched to touch him again. She knew what that skin felt like beneath her hands—the warm, almost velvet texture of it in contrast to the hard muscles beneath. She hadn't had nearly enough time to touch him, to explore him.

And she wanted to have that time. ASAP.

What in the world had happened to the focused, driven Nicola who'd driven through a storm with the sole purpose of catching a thief? Namely, Gabe Wilder.

She felt a lot like someone had caught her. And she wasn't doing nearly enough to break free. A sliver of panic helped her to drag her gaze away and she moved to the pile of robes still lying on the floor. But just looking at them had her blood heating all over again. And suddenly she could feel him looking at her. Every nerve in her body tingled, and she simply couldn't prevent herself from turning to meet his gaze.

And then she wanted to run to him—just as she had that day in the office. The longing was so intense that she could hardly bear it.

The sound of the helicopter came again, this time closer.

"What are we going to do about this? We can't—"

The reckless gleam in his eyes told her that they could.

Trying desperately to ignore the thrill that moved through her, she said, "They're landing. We have to clean this place up."

When he simply nodded and bent down to gather some of the robes, she let out the rest of the breath she'd been holding. Quickly, she began hanging what he handed her in the closet and ruthlessly shifted her thoughts to what she should be thinking about. Maybe if she could keep her hands and mind busy...

"Your father has to play a part in it, too," she said. "But this thief or group of thieves is doing two things differently. They send warning notes and strike only on holidays. Why?"

"Warning notes are ego related. A look-at-how-smart-I-am kind of thing. Holidays make the thefts more of a challenge. More fun." Gabe located a broom and began to sweep up the broken glass and flowers. "Makes more of a splash in the press."

"And you said your father always visited you and your mom on holidays. That's another connection to you and your dad." She turned to him from the closet and met his eyes. "Who hates you that much? And how did they get hold of the statue your father made?"

"I don't know. For that matter, I don't know who hates my father enough to rake all this up. Whoever it is had access to a specific statue that was in my mother's art studio the day my father was arrested. There should be a way to trace what happened to it. And I'm pretty sure the person I fought with tonight was a woman."

Nicola's eyes widened. "A woman?"

"Yeah. I fell on top of her at one point."

She was thinking again. Gabe could tell by the little furrow that had appeared on her forehead. He could almost hear the wheels turning. It wasn't just fresh eyes she was bringing to the case; it was a sharp mind and good instincts.

He didn't like to make mistakes, but he was pretty sure he'd made one by avoiding her for the past three months. He not only wanted her, he wanted to work with her on catching the thieves. Plan A was shot to hell and it was time for Plan B.

"What are you thinking?" he asked.

"Any chance this woman is working at G. W.?"

He picked up the last robe, then joined her at the closet door to hang it up. "My second in command at G. W. is a woman—Debra Bancroft. She's been with me since shortly after I started the business. Earlier this evening she was doing a walk-through of the security we've installed for the annual Valentine's Day Charity Ball at your family's home. Your father will be able to vouch for her." He'd arranged for Debra to handle the meeting with Nick and Marcia Guthrie because he'd been sure that Nicola would be there.

"Mary Thomas, my father's administrative assistant, would know all the details of the case," Nicola said. "She's been with him for over ten years, and she knows everything my dad knows. And Mark Adams has worked right at my dad's side from the get-go on this case."

Surprised, Gabe tilted her chin up so that she had to meet his eyes. He hadn't expected her to mention anyone in the FBI office. "I'm going to take issue with something you said before."

"What?"

"You said you didn't think you could be objective. I think you can."

She raised a brow. "If we're being totally objective, how can you be so sure that I'm not the one who cleaned your clock and then had my partner steal your car while I came back in here to play nurse Nancy?"

"Oh, I can be sure of that," he said with a grin. "The person I wrestled with is taller and had a good twenty pounds on you."

This time the sound of the helicopter was closer and louder.

"Our ride is landing." Then Gabe did what he'd been aching to do. He leaned in quickly to steal a short kiss. At least that was his intention, but it changed when her lips softened beneath his and her hands gripped his shoulders. He sank into her then, absorbing her flavors—that honeyed sweetness with a surprising bite that lingered and lured. He changed the angle, nipping lightly.

She trembled, but she didn't pull away. Neither did he. As the moment stretched, he was no longer sure he could.

Nicola told herself that she had to put a stop to the kiss. But it was so different from the others they'd shared. There was no shock, no blast of heat. Just a warmth that was even more seductive. And she had to figure this out. She had to understand how he could do this to her. How could he make everything else fade to the background until there was only him?

No one had ever done that to her before. No one had ever been able to make her want this way. To need this way. And as he deepened the kiss slowly, persuasively, the soft, drowsy warmth slipped seamlessly into an ache that built and built until it penetrated, not merely her body, but her mind and soul as well. She felt parts of herself slipping away.

He eased the pressure on her mouth enough to whisper, "Nicola?"

She knew what he was asking. He wanted her to let go and to tumble with him again wherever the moment would lead. She wanted to and knew she couldn't. There would be people knocking at the door of the church any minute. But there was a part of her that just didn't care. For a moment longer, she hesitated, letting practicality and common sense teeter on the brink with passion and the promise of delight.

Then the pounding came, muffled but insistent.

She drew away. "I can't. We can't." But she had to fist her hands at her sides to keep from reaching out and pulling him back. She made herself meet his eyes. "We can't make love."

Not right now. Gabe didn't say the words out loud. But they formed a drum beat in his head. He felt as if he'd taken a fast ride down a roller coaster without being strapped into a cart. He'd known she'd be different for him. Now he was beginning to suspect that she might be everything. Something sprinted up his spine. Fear?

She turned and led the way out of the room and down the aisle to let their rescuers in. He'd been right about the complications. Not only did he have a very clever thief with a special vendetta against him, now he had to figure out what to do about Nicola Guthrie.

7

AT SEVEN-THIRTY the next morning, Gabe faced Nick Guthrie across the wide expanse of a gleaming mahogany desk. The only thing that lay on top of it was the morning's paper with a headline that read: G. W. Securities and FBI Join Forces to Foil Attempted Robbery of Famed Statue of St. Francis.

"How's your head?" Guthrie asked, his gaze straying to the Band-Aid that now adorned Gabe's forehead.

"Good. I had one of my men escort Nicola home, and I stopped by a hospital where an old friend of mine works. She checked everything out, and aspirin should take care of any lingering effects."

Unfortunately, there was no such easy remedy for what he was feeling about Nicola. Sending her home with one of his men had turned out to be the most difficult decision of the evening. He simply hadn't wanted to let her go. Oh, he'd justified it rationally by telling himself that it was the smart thing to do. Because if he'd gone home with her, he wouldn't have let her go into her apartment alone.

And he'd needed to think, to sort through all the implications of what had happened at the church.

He'd done the right thing. But not all the rationalizing

he'd done had make it possible for him to stop thinking about her. And he hadn't once been able to rid himself of the desire to just throw caution to the wind and go to her. Even now, he was wondering when she'd arrive at the office, when he would see her again. He felt a bit like a teenager with raging hormones.

At the end of a long, sleepless night, he'd come to one conclusion. He wanted her to work with him on this case. Even though his motives weren't entirely related to catching a thief.

"You were lucky," Guthrie said.

Gabe met his eyes. "I might not have been so lucky if it hadn't been for your daughter's arrival."

"Nicola should not have been there. Neither should you." Nick Guthrie tapped a finger on the newspaper that lay between them. "Tell me that you did not have anything to do with leaking this story."

Gabe smiled. "That's a rhetorical question, right?"

Guthrie ran a hand through his hair and sighed. "Shit. Just tell me why. And while you're at it, tell me why you decided to use the statue of St. Francis as bait when we've put all our resources in place to catch this thief at the Valentine's Day Charity Ball tomorrow night?"

Gabe studied Guthrie for a moment. He was a tall, lean man in his late fifties who had the preppy kind of good looks that aged well. He knew that Guthrie's stellar record at the bureau had a lot to do with his being a meticulous planner. He always took the time to dot his I's and cross his T's.

The fact that Gabe hadn't filled him in on the prototype of his new alarm system and hadn't given him a heads-up on his hope that the thief might make a try for the statue was not sitting well with him. Gabe hadn't expected it to. Nick Guthrie didn't like to be thrown curve balls. Who did?

"You haven't talked to Nicola then?"

Guthrie frowned at him. "She's due in at eight. I'll see her after she types up her report."

A real I-dotter, Gabe thought. But he was beginning to get a clearer picture of Nick Guthrie's working relationship with his daughter.

"You still haven't answered my question," Guthrie said. "Why did you set up the statue of St. Francis as bait?"

"I wanted to rattle a cage or two. These thieves began by hitting us hard—a sort of one, two, three punch. Thanksgiving, Christmas and then New Year's. They'd stolen three pieces of art and broken through three of my alarm systems before I had an opportunity to analyze the problem fully. Then we had to wait a month and a half to see if they would strike on Valentine's Day. I figured the St. Francis might complicate their plans a bit."

"Why did you think they'd take the bait?"

Gabe shrugged. "The statue has a very high profile. There are plenty of people in the Denver area and beyond who believe in its prayer-answering power—and that makes it saleable to some collector. Plus, G. W. Securities installed the alarm system. I wanted to see if that would add to the temptation. I think it did."

"But in spite of the risks you and my daughter took, we still don't have anyone in custody. What if they're so *rattled* they skip the Valentine's Day Charity Ball? Where are we then?"

"Then we'll wait until St. Patrick's Day. Or Easter. But I don't think they'll skip the ball. They haven't missed a major holiday since this whole thing began. They even went for the St. Francis on a minor holiday. And failed. That's part of the reason why I leaked the story. After a well publicized failure, stealing the Cézanne that will be auctioned at the ball will be a matter of pride."

Guthrie rose and paced to the window. "I hope you're right."

"So do I. I miscalculated. I thought they'd wait until Valentine's Day to try for the St. Francis."

Guthrie turned and met his eyes. "You thought they'd go for both at once?"

"That's what I was hoping."

"And you would have been lying in wait at the church while everyone else was at the ball."

"Something like that. The security at the ball tomorrow night is tight. It's not going to be as easy as the other three robberies. Whoever is behind this is smart. They're going to protect themselves. We could end up preventing the theft but not catching anyone. I thought there might be a better chance of actually apprehending one of them at the church. But I didn't take into consideration that yesterday was Lincoln's Birthday."

"Hmmph." As Guthrie continued to stare out the window, the silence stretched between them.

And Gabe suddenly knew that Nicola had arrived for work. Every nerve, every cell in his body snapped to attention. He didn't bother to turn around. With the privacy shades drawn, he wouldn't be able to see her. But an image formed in his mind of that first time he'd spotted her stepping out of the elevator and striding purposefully to her office. She'd be wearing a neat business-like suit. And her hair would fall so straight into that slight curve. Neat. Way too neat. He couldn't help but wonder how many times he would have to run his fingers through it to tease back those curls? He hadn't yet had time to do that, and he badly wanted to.

"Earth to Gabe."

Gabe opened his eyes, shocked to find that he'd closed them.

"What are you thinking?"

Gabe quickly reined in his thoughts.

"Because I can tell you what I'm thinking. You and Nicola should never have gone into that situation at the church without backup."

"I sent Father Mike here to show you the note. When you weren't here, Nicola provided the backup I needed. She shot the perp."

"She shot the thief?" Guthrie strode back to his desk. "You didn't mention that when you talked to me last night."

"We didn't discover the blood until after I called you, and we'd already scheduled to meet this morning so that I could fill you in on all the details."

Guthrie sat down. "What the hell else haven't you told me?"

Gabe began the updates, starting with the fact that two men from G. W. that he trusted were on the scene at the church, getting a blood sample for DNA testing. One of them had even traced the abandoned car that Nicola had spotted in the ditch. It had been stolen and was free of prints. "Any news yet on my car?"

Guthrie shook his head. "I've asked the police to keep me updated. There were a lot of accidents last night, and attention has been focused on rescuing and treating victims. If your car was in one of them, I'll get a phone call. Eventually. Between the weather and the gunshot wound, our thief may not have made it back here."

"I've got a couple of my men running down gunshot wounds at the hospitals."

"Good." Guthrie met his eyes. "Anything else you haven't told me? You always save the best until last."

Gabe told him about his own signature being on the forged statue.

"Where is the forged statue now?"

"I have it safe at my place."

For a moment Guthrie said nothing, and when he spoke his tone was neutral. "So now we can be pretty sure that more than one person is involved in these thefts, and at least one of them is probably female. And the forgery this time has your signature on it. Where the hell did they get it?"

"The last time I saw that statue it was in my mother's art studio, the same place you found the Matisse that my father was arrested for stealing."

Guthrie frowned. "Any artifacts the FBI confiscated when they conducted their search were put in an evidence locker. Your mother's paintings were eventually authenticated and returned. The Matisse your father stole was returned to the museum."

The Matisse had been part of an exhibition that had been on a U.S. tour from a gallery in Madrid, and a year earlier, it had been stolen from an art museum in San Francisco. His father's initials had been on the forgery that was left behind. At the trial he'd denied both the theft and the making of the second painting. But the evidence had been overwhelming.

Nick Guthrie took a notebook out of his desk and picked up a pen. "I'll look into it."

After scribbling a few notes, he met Gabe's eyes. "And this forged statue with your signature makes you strongly suspect that someone in my office is involved."

"Whoever is behind these robberies had to have known that it existed and they also had to have access to it."

Guthrie leaned back in his chair. "That's the real reason you didn't fill me in on the prototype, and it's also why you requested to meet with me alone this morning before you filled me in on all the details. I have to be your prime suspect."

If there was one thing Gabe admired about Nick Guthrie, it was his ability to hide his emotions and keep his focus on the case.

"There's only one person I trust at this point," Gabe said. "Besides you."

"Who?"

Gabe had thought long and hard during the night about the best approach to take. Now, he chose the most direct one. "I trust Nicola, and starting right now, I want you to make me her assignment."

Guthrie leaned back in his chair and narrowed his eyes. "Why should I do that? She's an inexperienced agent."

"As far as I can see, she handled herself well last night. As for why you should assign her to this case—there are two reasons. First, someone is trying very hard to pin these robberies on me. The fact that they left that forged statue behind suggests that the St. Francis might have been on their to-steal list all along. If they'd been successful last night, you would have had to arrest me. So if Nicola watches me twenty-four-seven, you cover the bureau's ass—in advance. The second reason is the more important. She's already involved in this. The thief was not going to get the St. Francis. But she may have thought she could, given enough time. Nicola and I prevented that. And Nicola shot her. That news is bound to get out. Nicola's name is already in the paper. The fact that she shot the thief will be in the report she types up. Whoever is behind this is not going to be happy that a key member of their team is out of commission, and they may blame Nicola. These thieves haven't had much experience with failure up to this point. So far, everything has run like clockwork. Until we're sure how they're going to react, I say we take precautions."

"You think she's in danger?"

He met Guthrie's eyes very steadily. "I hope not. There's

been no violence yet. But I'd rather be safe than sorry. I don't want her out of my sight until this is over. Assign me to her and she'll be under the protection of G. W. Securities, and you have eyes on me. If I'm wrong, you still get eyes on me until we have somebody behind bars."

"Shit."

It was only the third time Gabe had ever heard Nick Guthrie swear. And all three times had been since he'd walked into the office this morning.

Guthrie ran his hands through his hair. "All right. Until this is over, you're Nicola's assignment." Then his eyes narrowed. "Promise me you'll keep her safe."

"Done." Gabe rose and held out a hand. "You won't be sorry." Then he said a quick prayer to St. Francis that he would make good on his promise.

8

NICOLA TAPPED THE PRINT BUTTON on her computer. It was 8:00 a.m., and she'd finished the report on what had happened last night at St. Francis Church. Through the glass wall of her office, she could see the papers shooting out of the printer that sat just to the side of Mary Thomas' desk.

Filing the report had been the assignment Mary had given her when she'd arrived a little after 7:30 to find that her father was already in a meeting behind closed doors. And in spite of the fact that he'd lowered the privacy shades, she was pretty sure she knew who was in there with him—Gabe Wilder.

She'd felt him right down to the marrow of her bones. Even right now, she was tingling in anticipation that she might see him again—much the way she'd felt on those long ago Saturday mornings when Marcia would drive her to the St. Francis Center.

At first she'd suspected that special agent Mark Adams was with them. But when he'd arrived at 7:45 and gone straight to his office, she'd felt better. At least she wasn't the only outsider. Mark was a tall, dark-haired man in his late thirties, and he'd been working with her father for nearly a decade. That meant he was a good agent.

She shifted her gaze back to the door of her father's office. When she'd told Mary that she should be part of the meeting, the woman had given her a sympathetic smile and explained that her father wanted her report on his desk ASAP. Then he'd see her.

So she'd written it up, and now she was back to square one.

She'd been so sure that last night would have made a difference. And if she'd caught the thief, it would have. But all she'd done was prove her father's theory that Gabe Wilder wasn't behind the robberies. But he was still at the center of it. She was sure of that.

And someone in this office might be involved.

Through the glass wall of her own office, she watched Mary stretch one arm gracefully to retrieve her report from the printer then place it neatly in her out-box.

Mary Thomas certainly fit within the parameters of Gabe's description of the female thief he'd wrestled with, but her father's administrative assistant gave no indication she was recovering from a bullet wound.

She figured the tall attractive brunette had to be in her late forties or early fifties, but she could easily pass for five or six years younger. And she'd been her father's trusted administrative assistant for almost fifteen years. In the three months since Nicola had joined the Denver office, she'd learned that Mary had a meticulously organized mind and ran a very tight ship. She also did yoga and tended to dress like a fashion plate.

Not that she had seriously suspected Mary Thomas of being the woman she'd shot last night. But the woman could be an accomplice—she knew everything that was going on in the Denver office's white-collar crime division. So could

Mark Adams. Her gaze drifted back to the man whose office was directly across from hers. And Debra Bancroft, Gabe's trusted assistant, could also be added to the list of possible suspects. If the robberies were a group effort, as Gabe was certain they must be, there could be more than one woman involved. After all, art theft and forgery were equal opportunity professions.

She glared at her father's closed door. So was the FBI. Supposedly.

Biting back a sigh of frustration, Nicola rose and paced to the window of her office. The sun was bright in the sky, and the snow had already begun to melt.

The instant she'd seen the headlines in the paper, she'd called Father Mike and left a message. Making the call had given her something to do. So had writing up the report for her father. And focusing on the case was the only way that she'd been able to get her mind off Gabe Wilder, however briefly.

She simply couldn't forget the kiss they'd shared just before they'd left the church and boarded the helicopter. In a way, that kiss had been more worrisome than making love to him. A onetime fling brought on by adrenaline and lust was almost understandable.

But the kiss had been different. There'd been a moment, however brief, when she'd felt as if she were coming home.

Talking about it had been impossible in the helicopter even if she'd wanted to. And Gabe had arranged for two cars to meet them at the landing pad. He'd said that he intended to stop by a hospital and get the cut on his head attended to.

She could hardly argue with that. But she'd wanted to. When the driver of one of the cars had driven her home and escorted her to her door, she couldn't help but wonder if Gabe had seen her to their door, would they have shared another kiss? Would they have gone inside and made love again?

And why couldn't she stop thinking about doing just that?

Seriously annoyed, Nicola strode to the counter behind her desk, opened a small refrigerator, and pulled out a caffeine-laden soft drink. Making love again with Gabe Wilder should be the *last* thing she wanted.

After twisting the cap off of the plastic bottle, she took a long swallow. He wasn't her prime suspect anymore. They should both be focusing on who was behind the thefts. Sending her home in a separate car had been an excellent move on his part. Obviously, they were returning to their first strategy—treating what had happened between them as spilled milk.

Fine. She was about to take another swallow of her drink when there was a knock at her door.

When she saw it was Father Mike, she set down her drink and hurried to let him in.

"You're all right." He took her hands in his. "Gabe assured me of that when he called me earlier, but when I received your message, I thought I'd come in person and see for myself."

"I'm fine." Nicola drew him toward a chair. He wasn't tall, and in spite of the fact that he had to be close to eighty, he moved with the agility of a much younger man. His hair was snow-white, and he had the kindest blue eyes she'd ever seen. When she'd first met him years ago at the St. Francis Center, she'd thought of them as Irish eyes because they always seemed to be smiling.

He drew a newspaper out of his pocket. "The statue is safe, but the thief got away. Gabe didn't give me much more than the paper has."

Quickly, she gave him a severely edited version of what had gone on in St. Francis Church the previous evening.

"Good thinking to use choir robes to prevent him from going into shock," Father Mike said.

Nicola could feel she was blushing. She'd of course deleted completely the part where she had decided to crawl in with Gabe.

Don't go there, Nicola. Stick to the case.

"Father, you've known Gabe for a long time, haven't you?"

"Since he was a baby. I was his mother's confessor."

She told the priest about her theory that Gabe was somehow at the center of why the thefts were occurring. "Do you have any idea of why someone would want to frame him for the thefts? Or to hurt him in some way?"

Father Mike leaned back in his chair and steepled his fingers. "Revenge is a powerful motivation. It's usually triggered by love or money. Sometimes both. A man in Raphael Wilder's profession—as good as he was—had to have made enemies."

She frowned as she thought about it. "A thirst for revenge that would extend from father to son...and then there's the money. Gabe says it's about the art, too."

Father Mike smiled. "You like him, don't you?"

Nicola frowned. *Like* him? Like seemed far too tame a word for what she'd come to feel about Gabe Wilder in the past twelve hours. "I haven't had time to think about that. Until last night at the church, I was sure he was behind the thefts."

"But you've changed your mind."

"Yes, he's not the thief."

"But he might have been if it weren't for you."

She stared at him. "What do you mean?"

"Fifteen years ago, you came into his life when he was at a crossroads."

Nicola frowned. "I was ten, and I let him tempt me into playing basketball instead of weeding the garden as I was supposed to do." And last night she'd let him tempt her again.

Father Mike beamed a smile at her. "Exactly. Teaching you to play and sharing his skill with you helped him to choose the right path." He tilted his head to one side. "And playing with him helped you also, I think."

"Perhaps." She met Father Mike's eyes. "You asked me if I liked him. I'm not sure I did like him when I was ten. But he fascinated me."

"And now?"

He still did, she realized.

Leaning toward her, Father Mike patted her hand. "If the two of you work together on catching this thief, you'll figure it out."

"Father Mike."

They both turned to see Mary Thomas standing in the doorway. "I buzzed Agent Guthrie that you're here, and he said to come right in."

Nicola rose when Father Mike did and walked with him to the door.

Mary said to her, "I'll check with him and see if he's ready to see you also."

Father Mike turned and took her hands in his again. "St. Francis will help you settle everything. You just have to have faith in his power."

For one long moment, Nicola stood in the doorway watching Father Mike disappear into her father's office. It didn't look as though working with Gabe on the case was going to be an option unless she figured out a way to make it one. And if she did, how on earth was she going to handle the intense attraction she felt for him? Still, she was debating whether or not to just follow Father Mike into her father's office when her phone rang. She hurried toward it hoping it was her father requesting her presence. "Agent Guthrie."

"Nicola, where are you?"

Nicola recognized the voice instantly. Her stepmother. And the call could only mean one thing. She was on Marcia's to-do list for the Valentine's Day Charity Ball. "I'm at the office."

"You have a meeting with Randolph Meyer this afternoon at 4 o'clock for a fitting of your gown. You can't miss it. You'll have to leave the office early."

Nicola didn't bother to argue that she *could* miss the appointment. The words would be wasted because Marcia, as much as she loved her, had a one-track mind.

"I want you to look perfect. Everyone who is anyone is going to be at the ball. I've had three people call today to ask if I can fit them in."

It wasn't nerves or annoyance that Nicola heard in her stepmother's voice. It was delight and excitement. Marcia loved to throw a party. And between the Cézanne that was being auctioned and the media buzz that an attempt might be made to steal it, the Valentine's Day Charity Ball had become a hot ticket.

"And Randolph is looking forward to seeing you again," Marcia said.

Meyer was *the* hot new designer that everyone in Denver's most elite social circles was using. Nicola also suspected that her stepmother had added Randolph to the list of eligible bachelors Nicola should be getting to know.

"Since you don't have an escort tomorrow night, I've invited Randolph to join our table."

Bingo, Nicola thought. Randolph Meyer would make

bachelor number four or five. She'd already lost count of the number of men Marcia had introduced her to since she'd returned to Denver.

"Yesterday, he stayed after my fitting and helped me make the decision on the desserts for the ball. Such a well-mannered young man. And so talented."

"What did you choose for the desserts?" Nicola asked, hoping to distract Marcia.

"Chocolate covered strawberries, chocolate cheesecake, crème brulee for those who avoid chocolate, and a selection of petit fours."

"Excellent. You always make just the right choices."

"But I won't be doing them forever, and you will have to step into my shoes. The charity ball has been held at the Thorne mansion for nearly a quarter of a century."

Nicola had heard the speech before, so she repeated her usual answer. "And that's where it will continue to be held. When the time comes, I'll step into your shoes, Marcia." She might not be able to fill them or meet all of Marcia's expectations, but she could certainly make sure that the annual ball went off on schedule.

"And you'll make the fitting with Randolph?"

To avoid answering the question, she lied. "I have another call coming in. I have to go."

She disconnected her stepmother and was replacing the receiver in its cradle when she suddenly tensed. Every nerve in her body began to tingle.

Gabe Wilder was here. She raised her gaze to meet his and just like that her pulse began to race, her nerves tingled.

He stood leaning against the door frame and she had to grip the arms of her chair to keep from going to him. He wore black from head to foot—slacks, turtleneck sweater and a leather jacket. And his eyes—at this distance—were nearly black, too.

Just looking at him made her want him. Desperately. It was that simple, that basic. That terrifying. No amount of common sense or practicality could control her instant and primitive response to just seeing him.

"Ready?" he asked.

She wasn't at all sure she was. Not for him. But there was a gleam in his eyes that tempted her just as it had when she was ten. "For what?"

"To take me on as your new assignment? I've convinced your father that someone needs to keep a close eye on me since the mastermind behind these thefts seems to be very intent on framing me for the robberies. The job is yours if you want it."

"I do." Snagging her purse from her desk drawer, she headed toward him. She wanted the job all right. Now all she had to do was keep her mind on it.

Gabe's cell phone rang.

"Wilder." Then he listened. She could hear the rumble of a voice on the other end of the connection, but she couldn't make out the words.

"I'll be there in ten minutes," he said as her father and Father Mike appeared in the doorway of his office.

"The state police just called," Nick Guthrie said. "They found your car in a ravine about four miles from Denver. The driver—a woman—was airlifted to a hospital several hours ago. They assumed the car belonged to the driver and didn't get around to running the plate right away."

"She's at St. Vincent's," Gabe said. "One of my men just tracked it down. They didn't discover the bullet until she was in surgery so it didn't get reported right away. According to my man, she wasn't carrying any identification."

There was a beat of silence as Mark Adams appeared in

the door of his office. Nick Guthrie turned to him. "Mark, I need to fill you in." Then he shifted his gaze back to Gabe. "The two of you go and check the woman out. Get an I.D. on her. I'll arrange for a police guard at the door, and I'll get on that other matter we talked about."

Nicola said nothing until they were out of the building and he was opening the door of a low slung black convertible parked at the curb. The car was certainly in Gabe Wilder's signature color, but it was a sharp right turn from the black SUV she'd tailed. "How in the world did you persuade him to assign me to watch you?"

He gave her a sideways glance as the engine leaped to life with a purr. "I appealed to what matters most to him. I told him I thought you were in danger. I do, by the way. And I promised him I'd provide you with the protection you need."

Nicola's eyes narrowed. "So *you're* really assigned to *me* and not vice-versa."

"Not at all." He smiled at her. "It's a mutual assignment, Curls. And a perfect arrangement. You get to prove yourself in the field, and I get to work with the best mind the Denver FBI white-collar crime division has."

Nicola felt the warmth steal through her right down to her toes. But as grateful as she might be to Gabe Wilder for making the "perfect arrangement," it didn't slip by her that she was dealing with a very smooth operator.

9

GABE STOOD WITH NICOLA and a male nurse just inside the room where a young woman lay hooked up to several beeping machines. Just outside the door, Pete Walters, a young man who'd been working for him ever since he graduated from college, was talking to the policeman that had just arrived.

The nurse's name tag read *Sid*. He was in his mid-twenties with brown curly hair and a cherubic face, and in spite of his youthful appearance, he ran a tight ship. He wasn't about to leave them alone with the injured woman, nor had he been overly generous with the details of her condition other than telling them it was critical.

"Five minutes," Sid reminded them. "Then I'll have to ask you to leave."

"She looks so young," Nicola murmured.

That had been Gabe's first thought when he'd seen her. It was hard to estimate her exact age because she had enough bandages wrapped around her head to make her look like a nun. But he was guessing late teens, early twenties. Except for a bruise that had darkened around one eye, her face was free of injury, and there were no wrinkles. She had delicate features and the high cheekbones of a model. And something about her pushed at the edge of his mind.

Not recognition. For he'd never seen this woman before. He was sure of that. Just as he was pretty sure that she was the same woman he'd fought with the night before. The hospital sheets were tucked tightly around a tall, athletically built body. Gabe stepped to the foot of the bed to get a closer look.

"That's far enough," Sid said. "I agreed to let you see her. That's all."

Nicola pulled a notebook out of her purse. "I'm going to make a sketch of her. The FBI has a program we can run it through. We may be lucky enough to get a match."

Gabe watched out of the corner of his eye as she moved her pencil skillfully over the page. The strokes were quick, competent. Either of them could have easily taken a picture with a cell phone, but the sketch might prove more useful. At the very least it was distracting the nurse.

"You're good at that," Sid commented, his eyes on her sketch pad now.

Gabe moved closer so that he, too, could take a look. Sid was right. She was very good. As he studied what was taking shape on the page, he once more felt the flicker of something, some memory. But it was too dim, too far away.

"Do you have any idea how old she is?" Nicola asked Sid.

"We figure she's in her early twenties," Sid replied. "Do they give lessons in drawing at the FBI?"

"I studied art in college," Nicola said. "She must have been badly hurt."

"Lucky for her Dr. Cashman was on call. He's one of our most skilled surgeons. She suffered severe head trauma in the accident, but he was able to relieve the pressure on the brain."

"She's going to make it?" Nicola asked.

"We're working on it," Sid replied. "The coma she's in is induced. The surgical team hopes to bring her out of it in a few days. Then we'll see if there's been permanent brain damage."

"There's a chance of that then?" Nicola asked, not glancing up from her sketch.

"Always. But Dr. Cashman is hopeful that he relieved the pressure in time."

"What do you think of the likeness?" Nicola asked, holding up her notebook.

"Very good," Sid said.

"Thanks." She shot him a smile before she flipped to a new page. "There was a gunshot wound also?"

"Dr. Cashman removed a bullet from her shoulder. No artery was hit, and it missed the bone. The pain and the loss of blood may have factored into why she lost control of the car, but there's a good chance the storm also played a major role. Our emergency room was filled last night with the victims of weather-related accidents."

She wasn't only good at drawing, Gabe thought. She'd also found a way to set Sid enough at ease, so that he was giving them the information they needed about the mystery woman's condition.

"That's why the policeman and that security agent are standing guard, right? Because of the bullet? Is she in trouble?" Sid asked.

"We won't know for sure until we know who she is," Nicola said. "Did she have any personal effects on her?"

"No wallet or cell phone," Sid said as he moved to a small closet. "Just this." Removing a plastic bag, he passed it to Nicola.

Inside was a bracelet. Nicola removed it and held it up to the light. The chain was thick, finely crafted gold and there was a flat gold disc hanging from one of the links. The engraved initials read D.A. Gabe felt something flicker at the edge of his mind again, but the memory was still out of reach.

Nicola slipped the bracelet into the plastic bag and said, "I'll want to keep this. It could help us with the identification."

When Sid frowned, Nicola hurried on. "Do you happen to know what color her hair was? That could be even more helpful than the bracelet. The last thing I'd want for her is to come out of that coma and not have anyone here for her."

"I'll make a call," Sid said and hurried out of the room.

"And while he's doing that, I'll get her prints." Gabe grabbed one of the plastic glasses and gently pressed the young woman's fingers to it. Circling the foot of the bed, he did the same with a second glass, tucked both into his briefcase, and moved to Nicola. "Great idea to make the sketch."

"It's the first time I've had any practical use for all those art classes my stepmother insisted on."

"Good job." He noted the flush that spread to her cheeks. "You're talented at drawing. You're also good at questioning people." And instinct told him that she hadn't heard a lot of compliments in her life. He'd have to do something about that.

"I like working with you, Curls." Then he made a mistake and did what he'd told himself he wasn't going to do, something he'd been aching to do ever since he'd walked into her office. He touched her.

Not the way he wanted to. All he did was tuck a strand

of hair behind her ear, but the simple act of brushing his finger over her cheek set off an instant chain reaction. Her breath caught, and he felt it like a punch in the gut. When the pulse quickened at the base of her throat, his own leapt to match it.

She raised a hand and placed it against his chest, and the pressure of each one of her fingers triggered a torrent of liquid heat so intense that the reality around him faded.

Neither one of them moved. He'd never experienced such an intense awareness of another person. In that moment, nothing else mattered. Nothing else existed except Nicola. The realization baffled him. It frightened him. And fascinated him.

"I want you. I have from the first moment I saw you in the office," he murmured.

"I know. What are we going to do?"

Run like hell. That's what he'd been doing for almost three months. But that wasn't what he wanted to do anymore. He was leaning toward her, closing the distance between them when a voice said, "Blonde."

They dropped their hands at the same instant as Sid entered the room. "She has blonde hair."

It was Nicola who recovered enough to turn and say, "Thank you so much, Sid. And we're going to get right out of your way."

Just outside the room, Gabe stopped to talk to his man, Pete.

Nicola listened to him fill the young man in, but she didn't speak again until they were in the car and Gabe had pulled into traffic. By that time her heartbeat had steadied and she could think again. But she didn't trust herself to look at him. Not yet. "We're going to have to do something about what's happening between us. The spilled milk strategy isn't working."

"Spilled milk?"

"That's what you said at the church. Ignore it and it will go away. It's not going away. We were in a hospital room with a woman who's in an induced coma. Someone who tried to steal the statue of St. Francis. And I lost track of everything when you touched me. *Everything.*" Just as she had in the church. Just as she had that first day in the office.

"It's a mutual experience, Curls."

She kept her eyes on the road but gripped the armrest when he took a quick right turn. "We have to find out who that woman is and how she's connected to what's going on. And there's a clock ticking on this."

"Agreed."

"We don't have time for…what's happening between us. We can't afford to…"

"Make love again?" This time he turned left and then swerved to pass the car directly in front of them. "We're going to. Because we both want to."

She should argue with him. Tell him they wouldn't, they couldn't. But she'd be speaking lies—not only to him but to herself. Instead, she said, "We shouldn't."

"Probably not." He took another sharp left turn and earned a long honk from an oncoming car.

Nicola glanced in the sideview mirror and noticed a blue sedan make the same turn. "Is that car following us?"

"I'm finding out." For a few seconds, he zigged and zagged through traffic.

Nicola noted that the blue sedan was still in her sideview mirror.

"You know, we're not exactly cut out of the same cloth, you and I," Gabe said. "And you're the daughter of a man who's been good to me. Who's trusted me. I've spent nearly three months avoiding you because that was what I felt I *should* do."

Nicola looked at him then. His eyes were on the road, but his knuckles had turned white on the wheel. "Do you always do what you should do?"

There was just a hint of recklessness in the smile he sent her. "Not always. But I try when it counts. My mother made me promise on her deathbed that I would live my life within the law, that I would never follow in my father's footsteps. So I've kept that promise. I'm not saying I did it on my own. Dad made Uncle Ben my guardian, and I had Father Mike, the St. Francis Center and good friends. Your father kept an eye on me, too. When I was first starting out, he called me in to consult on cases. That helped G. W. Securities build its reputation. I *should* have been able to keep my hands off of you. But you're different for me, Curls."

Her throat was dry when she tried to swallow. She hadn't been able to keep her hands off of him either. And she wanted them on him again. "You're different for me, too."

And what an understatement that was. But it occurred to her for the first time that maybe they weren't so different from each other. Whatever rebellions she'd had in her life—playing basketball, joining the FBI—she'd accepted the transfer to Denver partly because she'd felt it was what she *should* do. Sure her main goal was to prove to her father by her actions that she'd make a good field agent. That way he'd worry less about her job choice. But she'd also known it would please both of her parents if she returned to Denver.

Gabe made another left, and she noted that the blue sedan followed them.

She turned her attention back to him. "You know, when

it comes to doing what you *should* do, I could be the poster girl." But there was a time when you had to make a choice between what you should do and what you wanted to do. She'd made a choice when she was ten because she'd wanted desperately to play basketball with Gabe Wilder.

Want seemed far too tame a word for what she felt each time Gabe Wilder touched her. But she'd already made her choice. "We'll make love again."

"We will."

"But our priority has to be to catch the thieves. What's happening between us can't interfere. This case is too important."

"We couldn't be more in sync. We'll just have to juggle our priorities. Hold on to your seat."

She did and the right turn he took was so sharp it made the tires squeal.

She glanced in the sideview mirror again. "They're still with us."

"See? Neither one of us missed that. We seem to be juggling okay."

She glanced up at the tall building and recognized the parking ramp they turned onto. "You led them right to your office."

He pulled into a space. "I did."

She looked at him then. "I didn't notice them on the way to the hospital. Were they following us then?"

"No."

"Three people besides my dad heard you say we were going to St. Vincent's. Mary Thomas, Mark Adams and Father Mike."

"I wanted them to. The attempted theft has made the papers. The woman in the hospital hasn't checked in with her colleagues, so they'll check out St. Vincent's. I've got Pete, one of my best men, outside the door. The policeman is his backup. If anyone makes a move to contact her, we'll have more than we have now. And we need more than we've got."

"And one of the people in my dad's office may have sicced the tail on us," Nicola said.

"Our minds are running in tune. And that's more than we knew before, too. The important thing will be to make sure they don't follow us when we leave here later."

The grin he sent her reminded her so much of the boy who'd taught her to play basketball that her heart took a little tumble. She pressed a hand against her chest as he climbed out of the car and circled to open her door.

Making love with him was one thing. They were both adults, perfectly capable of deciding to indulge in a sexual fling. She was going to have to remember that anything more than that was not on her agenda.

10

WHEN THEY STEPPED INTO the elevator that opened off the parking garage, Gabe put a key in a slot and then punched in a code. "We'll go to the G. W. offices first. I need to check in with Debra."

State of the art was Nicola's first thought as she stepped into a hall that bisected a maze of glass-walled rooms. The place reminded her of the set of a Spielberg futuristic movie, and it seemed to fit the man walking at her side to a T. Smaller rooms housed individual desks with computer screens. About half of them were occupied.

Gabe led the way to the opposite end of the floor where a larger room offered a view of the city. Five people were seated around a glass-and-chrome conference table but Nicola's eye was drawn to the tall woman standing in front of a wall-size TV screen.

"That's Debra?" she asked.

"Yes."

The moment the woman spotted Gabe, she signaled to one of the men at the table to take her place and picked up a newspaper as she left the room.

Debra Bancroft was very attractive, but not in a flashy way. Nicola guessed her to be in her mid-forties, but she moved with the grace of a younger woman. She wore her blond hair pulled back into a bun. Her black jacket and slacks, which managed to look stylish and business appropriate at the same time, revealed a slender, athletic body. It occurred to Nicola that Debra Bancroft fit the description Gabe had given of his opponent at the church last night just as well as Mary Thomas had.

And neither one of them was the woman she'd shot. That young woman was currently in critical condition and tied up to tubes in an intensive care unit.

"Gabe." When Debra's glance shifted to Nicola, Gabe made the introductions. Then Debra held out the newspaper. "Have you seen this yet?"

Gabe gestured to the Band-Aid on the side of his forehead. "I was there." He gave Debra a brief rundown on what had occurred starting with Father Mike's phone call and ending with their visit to St. Vincent's and the condition of the young woman.

"You're all right?" she asked.

"Yes."

"We've thought from the beginning that there has to be more than one person involved. If this young woman pulls through, she may be able to identify the others. Do you want me to assign someone to stand guard?"

Gabe shook his head. "I've already arranged that, and the FBI has notified the police. There was a uniform on the door when we left the intensive care unit."

Debra's eyes narrowed as she absorbed what Gabe had told her. "So one of the thieves is already in custody."

"In a manner of speaking."

"I'm assuming we go forward with our security plans for tomorrow night even if they may be one man down."

"Yes. In the meantime, Agent Guthrie is assigned to me twenty-four-seven."

At Debra's raised brow, he continued, "The FBI wants to cover all their bases. We did install the security on the statue of St. Francis and the other art pieces."

"They suspect that we may be involved?"

"In their shoes, I would, too."

Debra glanced at Nicola, then shifted her gaze back to Gabe. "Could I speak with you privately for a moment?"

"Until this is over, the FBI and I have no secrets."

Something flickered in Debra's eyes, and Nicola thought it was impatience or annoyance.

"When I did the walk-through to check the security on the Cézanne, I noticed that you've installed a new alarm system, one that I'm not familiar with."

"Just as an extra precaution."

"I was surprised when I saw it."

"It's a prototype I'm trying out. I figured this was a good time to pull out all the stops."

There was a beat of silence before Debra continued, her tone noticeably cooler, "Should we consider making any other modifications to what we've set up for tomorrow night?"

Gabe gave her an easy smile. "I'll be working upstairs in my apartment reviewing that very question. If there are any changes, I'll let you know."

Again Debra's eyes flickered as Gabe turned away. This time Nicola thought it was definitely annoyance. She waited until they were back in the elevator before she said, "She didn't like the fact that you didn't fill her in on the prototype."

"I'm having that problem everywhere. Your father didn't much like it either."

Nicola couldn't prevent the smile at his slightly aggrieved tone. "You didn't tell her about the forged statue."

"I told her everything that she needs to know."

And everything Debra Bancroft could have discovered from other sources. If she was involved in the thefts. "So there are only three of us who know about the second statue of St. Francis."

"Outside of the thieves. I want them to wonder about it."

Right, Nicola thought, and then she was distracted by the space she stepped into. It was a large open area with skylights overhead and a wall of glass that afforded the same view of the city she'd glimpsed on the lower floor. The inside wall sported floor to ceiling bookshelves except for the space that held a theatre-size flat screen TV.

Her gaze skimmed over an L-shaped leather sofa and matching chairs. Beyond that she caught the gleam of a black granite counter framing a kitchen that her step-mother's chef might envy. To the left of the elevator, a wrought-iron staircase spiraled to a loft with more skylights overhead.

She shifted her attention to the work space to her right as Gabe moved toward it. The desk faced the windows, and if the rest of the apartment spoke of luxury and indulgence, Gabe's office was a testament to high-tech efficiency. But it was the floor to ceiling whiteboard behind it that surprised her. It looked like the "murder boards" she'd seen on TV shows.

Moving closer, she studied the series of photos pinned to it. From left to right were newspaper pictures of the art pieces that had been stolen so far. And the last one was a photo of the statue of St. Francis that had been in last Sunday's paper.

She glanced at Gabe to see that he'd already lifted the prints off the plastic glasses.

"Can you modify that sketch you drew? Take away the bandages and add blond hair?"

"Sure." Fishing her notebook out, she did what he'd asked and then handed it to him.

"I'll upload it into my computer along with the fingerprints and start a scan."

"What else can I do?"

"Take a good look at the whiteboard and tell me what you see. I need a fresh perspective." He didn't bother to glance up from what he was doing.

He was all business again, and Nicola, for the first time, was eager to follow his lead. The board intrigued her.

"Tell me your thoughts as you go along," Gabe suggested. "I'm at the point where I'm seeing the same things, thinking the same scenarios."

"I know just what you mean." She stepped closer to the board and studied the photo of the first piece of art.

Then she skimmed through the newspaper report. "The Monet was taken while the Langfords were having Thanksgiving dinner with friends, specifically my parents and me. Their house showed no signs of forced entry. Since the painting was still on the wall, they thought the note from the thief was a practical joke. Until they called my dad."

"Your thoughts?" Gabe asked.

"The thief either had the security code or possessed the skill to disarm the alarm system. The house was empty." She turned to face him. "Someone·skilled at disabling alarms or someone who had access to the codes could have pulled this off alone. No inside man needed."

Gabe looked at the board and nodded. "I agree. They would have had to know that the Langfords had art worth the trouble and that they would be out of the house on Thanksgiving Day. But that's Research 101 for a good thief, and this one is very good. What about the next robbery?"

She turned her attention to the board. The photo was of

a lovely color print of a Degas that had been stolen from the Glastons. The newspaper headline read: Christmas Day Robbery in the Suburbs.

"The whole Glaston clan, twenty-four in all, was there eating dinner. The chef had hired in a catering service. At some point, the note was dropped through a mail slot in the front door. The painting was kept in a glass case with its own separate security system." She turned to Gabe, intending to ask about the alarm, but once she met his eyes the question faded away.

He was closer than she'd realized. So close that their bodies had nearly brushed when she'd turned. If either of them made the slightest movement, they would come into contact. And she could read the awareness of that in his eyes. What she should do was take a step away and put some distance between them, but when an ache in her belly blossomed, all she could think of was that if she stepped a little closer…or if he did…

His gaze lowered to her mouth and lingered for one long moment. The ache in her belly stretched into longing, and her heart began to beat so loud that the sound of it seemed to fill the room. Still, she didn't move. Neither did he.

"I really like your mouth," he said.

She was so close to him that his scent filled the air—soap and something so male, so right, that it made her mouth water. The temptation to step forward grew.

Still, she fought it. Making love again was not what they'd come here for. "You're interfering with my ability to think again."

"It's mutual, Curls."

The nickname had her frowning. "I don't have them any more. And you wanted my thoughts on the case."

"True."

They were in agreement, so why couldn't she make

herself turn back to the board? Or why didn't he? She had to get a grip on this.

"Maybe we both need a little something to tide us over." He leaned in quick and did what he'd been wanting to do, what he'd been aching to do since he'd left her the night before. He kissed her. Just a quick one, he promised himself. But the instant he covered her mouth with his, her response was so generous, her flavor so…necessary…that he was lost.

Sensations hammered at him, through him, until he was sure his blood began to sizzle. Her mouth burned on his like a brand, and the need inside of him built until it was so sharp, so jagged, it sliced right through to his soul.

He could feel parts of himself slipping away and fear slid up his spine. No woman had ever been able to do this to him.

Only this one.

It was that thought that gave him the will to set her away from him and step back. He drew in a deep gulp of air, but he wasn't sure he'd ever get his breath back again. And looking at her with her lips swollen, her eyes dazed, had desire cutting through him again. He clamped down on the urge to just grab her and finish what he'd started. "Well," was all he managed to say.

"Well," she echoed. She felt as if she'd been knocked flat and come close to being out for the count. He'd kissed her before. Shouldn't she have been more prepared? But once his mouth had touched hers, there'd been nothing else but him. Nothing.

No one had ever had that kind of power over her. Only this man. And she needed to think about that. Once her brain cells clicked on again. And she needed to think about something besides jumping him.

"The case."

They said the words together, and Gabe smiled at her. "Nice to know that our minds are as in tune as our bodies."

"It's our minds that we came up here to use." It gave Nicola some satisfaction that she was the first to break eye contact and turn back to the photo of the Degas. But it took her a moment to bring the picture into focus. "Because the family was at home, this job presented more of a challenge."

"But it still could have been a one-man job. My father could have pulled it off quite easily, I imagine."

"But your dad would have created his own forgeries. You don't think that's the case here."

"No. As I said, someone with my father's talent is rare."

"So, hypothetically, one person on the team is good at breaking through security, making the switch and then getting away. She may very well be the one who's lying in that hospital room. Another one is talented at French Impressionist painting. But is it a two-man team or are there more?"

"That brings us to theft number three," Gabe said.

Nicola turned her attention to it. The headline read: Third Holiday Robbery.

"The Baileys were celebrating New Year's Eve with three hundred friends, and they'd locked the Pissaro in a floor safe. The note was delivered to the front door shortly after midnight and the butler handed it personally to Mr. Bailey."

"I personally installed the safe and set up the security code a few days before the robbery. The Baileys wanted extra precautions taken. I also installed two cameras without telling the Baileys. The thief or thieves disabled them."

"Who did know about the cameras?"

"Your father was the only person I told."

Nicola frowned. "He didn't mention them to me, but he keeps meticulous notes, which means that Mary Thomas could very well have known about them. And Mark Adams has been working very closely with my dad on the case."

"Here at G. W., the technician I worked with knew about the cameras at the Baileys and so did Debra. Any professional thief worth his salt would have checked for them, but it would have taken time. And with all the people in the house, that would have raised the risk of discovery and failure."

She moved closer to the whiteboard. "So you think the New Year's robbery would have required an inside source, someone who knew what you'd installed."

"That kind of knowledge would have helped with all of them," Gabe said. "But for the New Year's heist, I believe there had to have been someone with access to detailed information about the security and the cameras."

Nicola narrowed her eyes as she looked again at the photos and the headlines and felt that tingle that always told her she might be on to something. "More than one inside source maybe."

"What are you thinking?"

She moved closer to the board. "These victims all travel in a very small world. And whoever the thieves are, they had to have a fairly intimate knowledge of the social calendars of the Langfords, the Glastons and the Baileys. The New Year's Eve bash would have made the papers, created lots of buzz, but the fact that the Langfords wouldn't be home for Thanksgiving or that the Glastons would be having a large family dinner on Christmas and would be hiring caterers... Someone who moves in those inner circles and doesn't work for either your office or mine might be providing information."

"I hadn't thought of that. Good job." Gabe settled his hands on her shoulders. "What else do you see?"

Nicola tried to ignore the warmth that moved through her at his words. He had an ability to reach her on so many levels. "There's obviously an escalation in the difficulty of the job and in the risk. The first one takes place in an empty house, but the homes get more and more crowded. And while the number of people and the chances for easier access are increased, there's also more risk of discovery. There will be close to a thousand people at Thorne Mansion tomorrow night."

"Your idea of escalation makes the attempt to steal the St. Francis even more of an anomaly," Gabe pointed out. "Its location was isolated. No one was supposed to be around."

"Yes. But you went out of your way to bring that to the thief's attention, making it very tempting."

"Anything else?" Gabe prompted.

She studied the photos. "Each piece of art is portable, and, St. Francis excepted, they're all French Impressionist paintings. Those were your father's specialty. Even though forgeries are left behind, the thief wants them to be discovered. Why? And why holidays? There has to be a reason for that, and I'm betting that connects to your father, too."

Nicola moved to the first picture. "Last night, she came for the St. Francis alone. And there's a possibility that she worked the first robbery alone. Why?"

Gabe narrowed his eyes. "Maybe she did it to prove something. To show herself and perhaps others that she could."

Nicola tapped a finger against the photo of the statue. "But that raises another question about why she went for

St. Francis alone last night. If they're a team by now, why did she decide to go solo?"

"She's young. Maybe being a team player isn't what she expected. And it's a good possibility because of her age that she's not the one in charge. And if the first robbery was a test she had to pass to show her abilities…"

Gabe took a step back and swept his gaze over the pictures again. "Maybe the first three robberies are all practice. Work out the kinks until the big job at Thorne Mansion on Valentine's Day. That would explain the escalation."

Nicola felt that tingling again. "If you're right, then the painting that's being auctioned tomorrow night may be just as important as you are. You said it was about the art, too."

"Your father says the Cézanne is the most expensive piece that's ever been donated for the Charity Ball."

"And my stepmother is expecting the biggest crowd she's ever entertained. Because of the other robberies, there is some expectation among the guests that they'll be on the scene when this thief is taken down. Or when a major piece of art is stolen."

She stepped closer to tap her finger on the photo of St. Francis. "And maybe the attempt on the St. Francis isn't an anomaly. Maybe it was part of the plan all along."

"How?"

She turned to face him then. "If the forgery with your signature on it had been discovered at the church, G. W. Securities might not be operating at the top of its game tomorrow night. You might well have been in jail."

For a moment, there was silence in the room except for the hum of the computers behind them. Then Gabe took her hands in his. "I like the way your mind works, Curls. I wanted to bring you here last night."

"You did?"

"Very much. But I thought I needed distance. Perhaps we both needed some distance. I didn't even dare drive you home myself because I would have asked to come in."

Nicola let out a breath. "I would have asked you in."

"As it was, I didn't find myself thinking clearly about the case. I couldn't stop thinking about you."

"I couldn't stop thinking about you, either. I don't understand it."

He raised her hands and brushed his lips over her knuckles. "I want you, Nicola, but I also need you working on this case with me."

This time she couldn't ignore the warmth, not when it streamed through her like a warm, slow-moving river. Her heart took that little tumble again. "We've got a long way to go."

"I think we do."

She narrowed her eyes as a little skip of panic moved through her. "I'm talking about the case. We've got some pieces, but there are pieces we're missing."

"I couldn't agree more. We have a ways to go on the case, too." Then to her surprise, he grinned at her, pulling her to him and swinging her around in a circle. "But we're making progress."

When he set her down, her head was still spinning.

He nodded his toward the humming computer. "We'll get there, Curls. Something will float to the surface. It'll happen when we're totally focused on something else. And I have an idea about what we could do."

Her heart thumped hard when he grabbed her hand again. She fully expected him to head in the direction of the spiral staircase. And she didn't pull back. She didn't even open her mouth to protest. Not even when she realized he was pulling her toward the elevator.

It wasn't disappointment she was feeling. Definitely not.

But she was beginning to think that he was much better at juggling their priorities than she was.

"Where are we going?" she asked as the doors slid shut.

"To focus on something totally different."

When the elevator dropped only one floor and opened onto a professional-size basketball court, Nicola's eyes widened. The honey-colored floor gleamed. Bleachers lined three walls, and scoreboards hung over the hoops at either end of the court.

"Wow!" She turned to face him. "You've come a long way since you played on that basketball court outside of the St. Francis Center."

Gabe grinned at her the same way he had that first day on the basketball court. Her heart took another little tumble.

"I'd say we've both come a long way, Curls. Want to play?"

"I'm not dressed for basketball."

"We can change. Locker rooms are to your right. I keep a supply of uniforms and shoes here for the kids. Some of them can't afford them, and there are always new ones showing up. I'll bet a boys' large or extra-large will fit you. And you'll probably find a pair of boys' shoes that will fit." Taking her arm, he steered her toward the locker room door.

"What kids play here?"

"When the St. Francis Center had to close down, Nash and Jonah and I started up a boys and girls club that operates out of a building a few blocks from here." He pulled a T-shirt and shorts off piles on a shelf, then located a few shoe boxes. "Try these for size."

"Sure," she said as he handed her shoes and clothes.

"Father Mike still helps out there during the week.

Sports are a big part of the kids' activity schedule, and since I already had this built, they play all their basketball tournaments here."

There were questions she wanted to ask, but she wanted to play basketball more. "I'll race you," she said before she turned and ran into a changing room.

SHE'D BEATEN HIM BACK to the court and was waiting for him at the far end holding a basketball in her hands. The borrowed T-shirt and shorts weren't a perfect fit, and she shouldn't look sexy in them. But she did—enough to dry his throat. He purposely took his time moving toward her so that he could take in the view, something he'd denied himself for nearly three months.

She wasn't tall, but what there was of her was mostly legs. He'd explored the length of them, experienced the strength of them wrapped around him. Even thinly disguised in borrowed high tops, her ankles were narrow, her calves and thighs shapely and slender. Watching them, watching her stride toward him quickly, purposefully, triggered something inside of him that was more than lust, more than heat. He felt both of those, but he also simply liked the look of her. And he liked seeing her here on his basketball court. Somehow she looked right.

"Ready?" she asked.

His lips twitched. It was the same thing he'd asked her on that first day. "For what?"

"This." She held up the ball and he braced to receive it. Then quick as a snake, she darted around him and sent the ball sailing. It tapped the backboard lightly and fell through the hoop.

"Good job," he said as he caught the ball on the rebound. He pivoted and streaked for the other end of the court.

She kept up with him, and when he was close enough to

try the shot, she dodged in front of him and stole the ball. By the time he turned, she'd raced away. Because she'd surprised him, delighted him, she had time to pause at the three-point line and sent the ball whispering through the hoop.

He ran right past her, snagged the ball as it fell, and ran with it. She was on him like glue. He sank his shot this time, but it was no easy thing.

She took the rebound and when he tried to block her, she turned into him and rammed her shoulder into his chest before running away.

"Foul," he called after her.

"I didn't hear a whistle." She executed another perfect layup.

He couldn't prevent the laugh, nor the admiration for her skill. Her guts. But he did play harder then. Sure he may have held back a little. And he may have let her get away with a couple of things that he definitely wouldn't have tolerated from his friends Nash or Jonah. But she could feint and fake as well as they could. Still, he was bigger, and he didn't want to send her crashing to the floor.

But overall, they were well matched, and she was a hell of a lot better at the game than she'd been when she was ten.

She was sneakier, too. Once, when he threw out an arm to block her, she ducked right beneath it and streaked away. Another time, he'd barely caught a rebound when she'd run in, leapt up and twitched it away with her fingertips.

She might have to take two steps to his one, but every-time he turned, she was there. And he wasn't the teacher anymore. Envy had streamed through him when he'd seen her take an over-the-shoulder hook shot.

Gabe lost track of time and eventually of everything but Nicola and the game. They were both panting when they finally stopped at midcourt to catch their breath. Air burned his lungs. And she still had the ball. He could tell by the look in her eyes that if he made a move, she'd be off like a shot. What a woman.

"I think…you won," he managed to say.

"I definitely…won." She straightened, drew in another breath. "But if there's…a question…" She turned, took one dribble, then sent the ball sailing. He watched it travel in a wide arc and then whoosh through the net.

"You're amazing. I'd like to think that I taught you everything you know."

She laughed then. Her face was flushed. Her hair, damp from sweat, had begun to curl. Hunger for her exploded inside of him. Though it had been thrumming through his system from the moment he'd stepped into her office earlier, it had never swamped him so quickly, so thoroughly before.

He moved in quickly, lifting her so that he could swing her around. By the time he'd turned in a full circle, she'd wrapped her arms and legs around him, and he felt every curve of her body mold perfectly with his. Their faces were aligned, their mouths a breath apart.

"I think this has to be a foul," she said.

"Thank God, there's no ref around."

He threaded his fingers into her hair and took her mouth with his.

11

GABE THOUGHT HE'D BE READY for her taste. But the moment her flavors exploded on his tongue, the blood drained out of his head so fast that he had to shift his feet to maintain his balance. Then he tore his mouth from hers and feasted on the skin at her throat. So smooth and salty with a lingering undertone of the soap she'd used. His hunger for her only grew.

The hitch of her breath, the sharpness of her nails—each sensation ignited a new craving. The voraciousness of his appetite stunned him. So did the very real fear that he might never get enough of her. That strong, slender body pressed against his felt so right. So necessary.

All he could think was more. More. He had to touch her. He ran one hand down her back and pressed her even closer. The heat they created exploded through him and nearly had him dropping to his knees.

Only then did he find the strength to pull back. She was still wrapped around him tight.

"I have a perfectly good bed upstairs." And hadn't he planned on using it? Hadn't he fantasized for nearly three months about using it?

Those glinting brown eyes met his. "I can't wait another second."

Neither could he. Yanking down her jersey, he fastened his mouth on her breast.

With an abandonment she'd never experienced before, Nicola arched against him, digging her fingers into his shoulders and calling out his name. She couldn't think. She didn't want to. All she wanted was to feel. She'd never wanted like this. Never needed like this.

Then they were on the floor, groping, grappling, fighting with clothes until they were naked. Fast and greedy, as if she were afraid that he might escape, she ran her hands over him, searching, seeking. And wherever he touched, her body burned with flames he not only set but stoked.

And none of it was enough. She had to have more. As if he'd read her mind, he used his mouth on her. Ravaging her breasts with teeth and tongue, then making a fast, torturous journey down her torso. She barely had time to absorb one sensation before another battered her system.

When he scraped his teeth against her inner thigh, she arched high. There was a tremendous ache building. And when his tongue pierced her center, so did a lance of pleasure so sharp, so consuming, that she lost her breath and some of her mind. As she spiraled slowly down from the peak, she was sure there couldn't be any more. But he showed her there was, building the pleasure again, pushing her higher and higher until a second climax dragged her over the edge.

Her breath was sobbing and he couldn't seem to catch his at all as he moved up her again. He could feel her trembling beneath him, but he saw only her eyes—just the dark glint of them watching him as he rose over her. Nothing else.

He wanted nothing else. Here was everything. The

thought pierced him as deeply as the pleasure when he thrust into her. She closed tight around him and for a moment neither of them moved. Sunlight streamed through the windows and dust motes danced. If he could have, he would have stopped time. More than anything, he wanted to hold her right here forever. When they began to move, it was together—rising, falling, sighing. Their breath mixed, tempting his mouth to take hers again and again as the tempo increased.

They made love then just as furiously as they had while playing basketball. Faster and faster until he felt himself surrender and slip over the edge. With his face buried in her hair, he let himself fall.

NICOLA DIDN'T WANT TO MOVE. And that didn't make any sense. They were lying on the hard wood of a gym floor, sweaty from sex and their game, and she'd never felt more comfortable.

But it was time to get back to finding the thieves, and it was high time that she became better at juggling their priorities. She drew in a deep breath, and when she smelled nothing but him, her thoughts very nearly scattered again.

Focus, Nicola.

She tried to move, but Gabe forestalled her by shifting so that they were facing each other, their bodies still tangled.

"Are you all right?" he asked.

"Yes, but I think that you definitely won the second round."

"It was my pleasure." He wound a strand of her hair around his finger. "I've always liked this room, but I'm never going to think of it in quite the same way."

Her lips twitched. "I may never think of basketball quite

the same way. My games don't usually end with wild sex on the floor. But it was fabulous."

He laughed, then gave her a quick kiss on the tip of her nose. "Agreed."

It took some effort, but she managed to sit up. Their scattered clothes looked like the aftermath of a war. "Well, I'd say we were very successful in shifting our focus away from the robberies. The question is, did it work?"

Neither said a word as they gathered their clothes. Nicola reviewed a mental list of everything they'd talked about while they were looking at Gabe's whiteboard.

"Sometimes the flash of insight doesn't come to me right away. It could come while we shower," Gabe said.

"Separate showers," Nicola said in a firm tone as she moved toward the locker rooms. "The scan may have produced some results. And I want to check out the Cézanne."

"Why?" Gabe asked.

She glanced back over her shoulder. "Because if our theory is right and the other robberies are a prelude to tomorrow night, I want to know everything about that painting."

A HALF HOUR LATER, Nicola once again felt that little tingle that told her she might be on to something. The Cézanne that was being auctioned off tomorrow night had a very short history of owners. An ancestor of the Robineau family in Denver had acquired several early works from the artist himself before leaving Paris and coming to the United States. But sixteen years ago, the Robineaus had lent their entire collection to the Denver Art Museum.

And there'd been an attempt to steal at least one of them.

"Bingo," she said as she brought up the newspaper story. Her stomach sank as soon as she noted the date.

"What?" Gabe asked as he turned away from the white-board.

"It may be nothing." And she wasn't sure how to tell him.

He moved behind her and scanned the screen. "An attempted robbery just after a gala launching the Cézanne exhibit...nearly sixteen years ago. After the party, the thieves concealed themselves in the museum, but set off a silent alarm. The police arrived on the scene, and when they made a run for it, one of them was shot and killed. Bedelia Bisset. At least one other got away in a van."

Nicola said nothing.

"You're thinking my father may have been her partner," Gabe said. "The one who got away."

"He was living here in Denver at the time."

"Yes. But in February 1995, my mother was still alive and very ill. And he'd made her a promise. That way of life was over for him."

She could feel the tension radiating off of Gabe in waves, and she could see a trace of pain in his eyes. He had to be wondering if it was a promise his father had eventually broken. Without thinking, she turned in her chair and took his hand in hers. His fingers gripped hers hard.

"He must have been questioned about the attempted theft of the Cézannes, don't you think? There's no mention of FBI involvement, but I could call my father and ask."

Gabe shook his head, then released her hand. "Not yet. There's someone else I want to talk to first. And we need to find out more about this Bedelia Bisset. I want to look at a photo of her."

"I'll get on that."

Just then the desktop computer stopped humming and gave a soft beep. They both turned to look at the split screen. On half of it the fingerprint scan was still running.

But on the other half was the driver's license of a young woman who looked very much like the sketch Nicola had drawn at the hospital.

"Claire Forlani," Gabe said as he tapped keys to print out a copy. Then he took out his cell and punched a number. "I don't want to turn this over to anyone here, so I'm going to have my friend Jonah Stone look into both Bedelia Bisset and this Claire."

Nicola heard the faint sound of the phone ringing.

Then Gabe said, "Jonah, I need a favor…"

Nicola studied him as he listened for a moment and then broke out into laughter. As the sound filled the room, she saw some of the tension leave his shoulders, and some of her own drained away with it.

Although they'd followed very different paths in life, it was clear to her that Gabe, Jonah, and Nash were still very close friends. She'd looked into both of them when Gabe had been at the top of her suspect list. Nash Fortune had left Denver to make a career for himself in the air force. He was currently stationed nearby at the Air Force Academy. Jonah now owned a string of successful nightclubs in San Francisco.

Nash's family was in Denver's social register. Jonah's wasn't. In fact, she hadn't been able to find any trace of family at all when she'd run the check on him. He'd been of special interest because he'd spent a few years helping Gabe establish G. W. Securities before he'd moved to San Francisco.

And if Gabe had been the thief and had needed a partner? Well, she'd figured Jonah might just be the man he'd choose…

Odd, she thought as she studied him. Gabe was sitting on the corner of the desk, his long legs stretched out and crossed at the ankles. Less than twenty-four hours ago, she'd been so sure that he had to be involved in the thefts. And he was, just not the way she'd thought. She glanced at the whiteboard again. The robberies themselves were turning out to be something other than what she'd thought, also.

But the tingle she'd felt a few minutes ago was telling her that there had to be a connection between the attempted robbery of the Denver Art Museum sixteen years ago and what was going on now. Was it just a coincidence that the Robineau family's collection of Cézannes had been on display in the museum and now one of their Cézannes would be auctioned at the Valentine's Charity Ball? She didn't think so. All she had to do was find more pieces to the puzzle.

"Okay, we'll have that weekend together. Just as soon as I tie up these robberies…no, I'm not going to mention any specifics over the phone. I'll send you details in an encrypted email. I do have some knowledge of how cell phones are tapped into."

As Nicola caught the sound of laughter on the other end, she rose and began to stroll down the length of the room. Curiosity drew her gaze to the books first. They ranged from bestsellers to the classics. She ran her finger down the spine of what looked to be a well-worn edition of the complete works of William Shakespeare.

There were photos, also. She moved toward the one of the Gabe Wilder she'd carried in her head all those years ago. He stood between a tall man who had to be his father and a fragile-looking woman. Her throat tightened. Then a flicker she caught out of the corner of her eye had her glancing at the two smaller flat screens on the far side of the big one. Each offered a different view of the offices below. Debra Bancroft was still holding her meeting in the large conference room, and several more of the smaller offices had filled.

She glanced back at Gabe who was now at the laptop, his fingers running over the keys. No, he wasn't a man to forget anything about security. Sending the names to Jonah in an email would be safer than discussing the case over the phone.

When he straightened, he glanced at her. "Ready?"

Her heart gave a little thump as she moved toward him. "For what?"

He tucked a strand of hair behind her ear. "Still the cautious answer. I told you I wanted to talk with someone before we fill your father in. So we're having lunch with an old and dear friend, my Uncle Ben."

The elevator doors slid open as they reached them. "I hope it's not too far. I'm starved."

"It's not far and the food is fabulous."

THE ONE THING SHE HAD to say about Gabe Wilder was that he was full of surprises. This time he'd made very sure that they hadn't been followed. Who would have thought to look for them in the beat-up truck he'd driven out of the parking garage? She'd been hiding on the floor of the front seat, and he'd put on another flannel Paul Bunyan shirt and some kind of cap that had been in the cab of the truck. Something very country was blaring out of the radio so loud she'd thought she might suffer some hearing loss.

It wasn't until they were speeding out of the city and into the hills that he'd allowed her to buckle into the passenger seat. She reached immediately to turn the volume down on the radio.

"Not to your taste?" he asked.

She shifted in her seat so that she could study him.

"You're enjoying this, aren't you? The disguise, the beat-up truck, the speed?"

He shot her a quick grin. "Yeah. Running G. W. Securities has gotten a bit boring lately. In the beginning, I got to do a lot of investigative work—insurance fraud."

"So you could put on a disguise and play a con?" she asked.

"Yeah. I guess that's why I could understand why it was hard for my father to give up the life he loved. I just try to keep my cons inside of the law."

"Did you inherit your affinity for Paul Bunyan shirts from your father, also?"

Gabe laughed, and Nicola found herself smiling at the sound.

"My Uncle Ben gives them to me for Christmas every year. It's his way of telling me that my wardrobe choices are too somber. I try to wear them whenever I visit him. I was on my way to see him yesterday when Father Mike called me and I headed to the church instead."

"This place is close to St. Francis Church?"

"It's about thirty minutes closer to the city. Uncle Ben lived in my mother's home until a year ago when he started having to use an oxygen tank. Then he announced he was moving out to this assisted-living home. The Eyrie. He's always been a gourmet cook, and he decided that if the oxygen tank was going to interfere with his ability to be creative in the kitchen, he was not going to give up eating gourmet food. I try to get out here when I can to share a meal with him."

"You think he might know something about this Bedelia Bisset."

"He might know if my father knew her."

Then she asked the question that had been in her mind ever since she'd found the information on the attempted theft of the Cézanne. "Are you going to be all right with what we find out about this?"

He glanced at her. "Yeah. I don't believe that my father had anything to do with that failed robbery at the art museum. If he had, they would have gotten away with it."

She said nothing.

"I don't believe he stole the Matisse that your father discovered when he searched my mother's studio. I think he was framed."

Framed. Nicola said nothing in reply, but she felt that tingle again. *Framed.* She turned the idea over in her mind as they drove farther into the mountains.

On the one hand, she could understand the unconditional belief in a loved one that would cause a boy of thirteen to insist on his father's innocence. But Gabe wasn't a boy anymore. He was smart, savvy—nobody's fool. And he had to have a very clear idea of what his father had been and what Raphael Wilder was capable of since he'd inherited some of those skills and honed them.

She put a hand to her stomach where the tingle was growing stronger. What if it wasn't wishful thinking or blind loyalty that made him so certain that his father had been framed? What if he was right?

And if Raphael Wilder had been framed for the theft of the Matisse, that might add another piece to the puzzle they were trying to solve now.

"Theoretically, how did they do it? Frame your father, I mean."

The look that he shot her held surprise. As he shifted his gaze back to the road, he said, "Your father's office received an anonymous tip telling them to check the Matisse at the museum in San Francisco. When they did, they discovered it was a fake and my father's initials were in the lower right-hand corner."

"The initials could have been forged."

"Yes. But the fact that they were there got your father the search warrant. And they found the real painting in my mother's art studio tucked behind some of hers. My father hadn't been able to bring himself to sort through any of her things yet."

"Did they discover when the Matisse was actually stolen from the San Francisco museum?"

"No. Whoever did it was good. The FBI's best guess was that the robbery might have taken place over a year earlier during Easter weekend when there'd been a small glitch discovered in the security system. But nothing had appeared to be missing. It might have been years before the theft was discovered—if not for the anonymous tip."

Nicola thought about that as Gabe made a right onto a drive lined with trees. A sign to their left read *The Eyrie.* "But your father never named anyone as a possible informant?"

Slowing to a stop in front of a long porch, Gabe shook his head. "Your dad let me read the file including all the transcripts of interviews with my father. He claimed to have no idea who might have called in the tip."

She turned to face him then. "No wonder you believe your father was framed. So do I."

He studied her for a moment. "Why?"

"Because it doesn't add up. If your father had stolen that painting, he wouldn't have brought it to your house. He especially wouldn't have hidden it among your mother's paintings."

"Your dad's theory was that he might have taken it before he'd promised my mother that he would give up his old life, and he was stuck with the painting. Maybe he was even planning on returning it."

Nicola couldn't help but wonder if her father had really

considered those possibilities or if he'd described them to comfort a thirteen-year-old boy.

"Or he was waiting for a certain time to pass after her death to go back to his old way of life," Gabe continued. "I don't believe that, but I can't prove it."

"If we find out who really stole that Matisse, maybe we can."

Gabe framed her face in his hands. He couldn't have named the emotions that she'd unleashed inside of him. The simple belief in her eyes and in her tone soothed away something that he hadn't even been aware of. "Thanks."

"For what?"

"For believing in my father."

"No. I believe in you. And the evidence. I researched Raphael Wilder. I read the file they had on him at Interpol. I find it hard to believe that someone with his reputation and skill would hide that painting where it might incriminate him. How hard would it have been for someone to plant it in your mother's studio?"

"Not hard at all if we're talking about the same person who got it out of the museum."

"It's connected to what's going on now. It's just got to be. Somehow. That Matisse had to be worth a bundle. If we're right, someone gave up a small fortune to put your father behind bars. And I think they're trying to do the same thing to you."

If we're right. The words sent a new flood of feelings through him. "I knew I needed fresh eyes on this." He leaned toward her then and brushed the merest hint of a kiss over her lips. "But I was wrong about that. What I needed was *your* eyes."

Her hands moved to his shoulders. His were still framing her face. And he was losing himself in her again. He watched her eyes darken, and in their depths he saw himself. Trapped. Hadn't he known he would be from the first time he'd looked into them?

Lord, he wanted to touch her. It seemed like forever since he had. His hands recalled the feel of her, the warmth of that skin, the silken texture. And his mouth recalled her taste, that mix of sweet and pungent flavors. And if he took her mouth now...

Just thinking about it had his whole body tightening because he knew now what her response would be—wild, free. And when her body was pressed fully to his, there would be that total yielding. That complete surrender. Then the world that was already dimming would slip entirely away.

He could feel her breath on his skin, feel it slip between his lips. It was his. She could be his. All he had to do was close that small distance.

The only thing that kept him from moving was the realization that if he did kiss her, he'd need more. And he might not be able to stop himself from taking more. His batting average in that direction was not good.

With a sigh, he leaned his forehead against hers. "I want to kiss you but I'm going to have to give you a rain check. Uncle Ben is waiting. We need a better place. A better time."

The breath she drew in and let out was nearly his undoing. "Rain check accepted. But finding that better place certainly hasn't been a priority for either one of us so far."

The hint of dryness in her tone had his lips curving. He drew back then and found the strength to drop his hands. "I'm going to have to put more effort into that."

THE EYRIE ASSISTED-LIVING facility lived up to its name. Like an eagle's nest, it was nestled right into the mountain.

The atrium boasted a lofty skylight and a glass wall that offered a stunning view of the surrounding mountains.

To Nicola, it resembled the lobby of a busy five-star hotel. One of the residents sat in a wheelchair in front of an easel. Others relaxed on leather couches reading books. Three corridors branched out from the circular space and at its center stood a white piano that might have made Liberace jealous.

"Uncle Ben." Gabe led her toward a tall man who was surrounded by women. When he turned and walked in their direction, Nicola could see why. Gabe's uncle was definitely a female magnet. He resembled Sean Connery, she decided. His height, his athletic body and his killer good looks were a stunning combination. And the oxygen tank didn't seem to slow him down any. It was one of those portable ones that he could carry over his shoulder.

The two men went into an easy, masculine embrace the moment that Bennett Carter reached them.

When they separated, Bennett let his hand remain on Gabe's shoulder for a moment. "You missed poker night last night. I'm assuming that whatever prevented your presence is connected to the Band-Aid on your forehead and that story in the paper this morning."

"Correct. It's fine. I'm fine. I'll fill you in on all the details after we eat. I want you to meet Nicola Guthrie. FBI special agent Nicola Guthrie."

Bennett took her hand and grasped it warmly. "He knows that I'm easily distracted by a beautiful woman. Is he fine?"

She smiled at him. "Very."

As he led the way into the dining room, he said to Gabe, "When I got your text, I reserved a table with a view and some privacy."

While they browsed the menu and made their decisions,

the two men talked on general topics. Nicola had ample time to study them. In spite of the age difference, which Nicola guessed to be about fifty years, there was an easy camaraderie between them that spoke of long acquaintanceship and family.

"Have you been back to the house lately?" Bennett asked.

Gabe picked up a roll, broke it and offered him a piece. "Too busy. Who would I visit at the house now that you're gone? Do you miss it?"

Bennett shifted his gaze to her. "He asks me that every time he comes here. And every once in a while, I do miss the peace and quiet." He winked at her. "But this place offers a lot of social networking possibilities."

"And Uncle Ben engineers most of them," Gabe commented.

As they continued to chat, Nicola turned her attention to the food, which had just arrived—a delicious tuna Niçoise that Bennett had highly recommended. Gabe had been right about it being fabulous, and Bennett had been right about the view. Through the wide glass window, the hills were crisscrossed by narrow, flat valleys. Patches of snow lay thick on the peaks and still blanketed the treetops in the green forests. The conversation lingered on general topics until the waitress brought their coffee.

As soon as she'd filled their cups, Bennett said, "How about those details now?"

Gabe filled him in on what had happened at the church the night before and everything they'd discovered since then. This time he left nothing out.

Bennett lifted his cup and sipped his coffee. "You want to know about Bedelia Bisset. That was the name in the newspaper coverage of the attempted robbery of the museum, but I knew her as Dee Atherton."

"Dee could be short for Bedelia," Nicola said. Digging into her purse, she pulled out the plastic bag that contained the bracelet she'd taken from the hospital. "The charm has the initials, D.A. Do you recognize it?" she asked as she tipped it onto the table.

Bennett picked it up and studied it. "Dee Atherton wore a bracelet like this. She told your father that her partner had given it to her."

"My father knew her?" Gabe asked.

"She worked with your father once in Paris, shortly after you were born. Your mother had already taken you back to Denver. Dee was very young, barely out of her teens, and she was very good at breaking through locks, safes, any kind of security. You name it, and she could get through it. Your father thought she had a real feel for it." Bennett met Gabe's eyes. "The same kind that you have. Except that you've used your talent on the other side of the law. Your father never worked with her again. He said she was impulsive, cocky, that she liked the rush almost as much as she liked to bag the prize. Your father, as much as he loved the game, was a meticulous planner, and something had almost gone very wrong during the job, something she hadn't warned him about."

Bennett raised his hands and then dropped them again. "I don't have any more details than that about Paris, but we ran into her four or five years later in Venice. She had hooked up with a new partner—an Italian, I think, and a very good forger. That was the first time I saw her wearing the bracelet."

Bennett sipped coffee before he continued. "She tried to convince your father to work with them. He turned her down."

Gabe studied his uncle for a moment. "What else?"

"She came to see your father again about a month before

the attempt at the Denver Art Museum. That would have been more than five or six years since we'd run into her in Venice. He spoke to her in your mother's studio. About a week later, she came back again, and she was carrying a long tube."

"Blueprints," Gabe said.

"That was my guess, too. It wasn't until the papers carried the story of her death that your father told me she'd come to ask him to help her steal one of the Cézannes from the collection. I'd surmised something like that. But he'd refused."

Bennett reached out and covered one of Gabe's hands with his. "He'd refused. He wasn't a part of it. He said he'd sent her away without looking at the blueprints. But he felt guilty about her death."

Gabe picked up the bracelet. "When I first saw this, it looked familiar to me."

"Makes sense," Bennett said. "After your mother died, you spent as much time as you could with your father in the studio. You may have seen her one of the times she came."

"There's more," Gabe said as he handed the bracelet back to Nicola. "I just can't remember it. Maybe I don't want to remember it."

Nicola studied Bennett for a moment, then asked, "Do you think Raphael Wilder stole the Matisse?"

Bennett hesitated.

Gabe covered one of Bennett's hands. "Uncle Ben isn't as sure about my father's innocence as I am."

Bennett met her eyes. "I'm not proud of the fact that I don't have as much faith in Raphael as Gabe does. And during that time frame when they believe the Matisse was stolen, Raphael was making some trips, tying up loose ends. What I do know is that he was determined to give up the life and settle down here. He loved Aurelia and Gabe very much."

"Uncle Ben thinks Dad might have stolen the Matisse as a last fling," Gabe said.

"He always denied it," Bennett said.

"It's all right," Gabe assured him. "I've always been the only one who believed in his innocence until I met Nicola here."

"Ah." Bennett reached for her hand then and gave it a squeeze.

"I have a question for you," Nicola said. "Why did Raphael take up sculpture?"

"That's an easy one. Aurelia, Gabe's mother, suggested it to him. She knew him very well. More than any of us, she realized what it would cost him not to go back to his old life. And he'd evidently toyed with sculpting while they were together in Paris. The next thing I knew he was ordering chunks of marble shipped over from Italy."

"Do you have any idea why he started with the St. Francis?"

Bennett shook his head. "I can't help you there."

Gabe took out his phone. "Jonah has something." He pushed a button, scanned a text. "Bedelia Bisset is an alias for Dee Atherton—Interpol's file on her lists her under both names. And he's sending a picture."

When he pressed the button, Nicola could see from his face that they had something. "What is it?"

"It's coming back to me. The memory has been tugging at me ever since we were at the hospital. I did see her when she came to the studio. And both times, my dad sent me out into the garden to play."

Gabe turned his cell so that both Bennett and she could see the picture Jonah had sent.

"That's Dee Atherton," Bennett said. "I'd swear that's her."

Nicola just stared at the image. Though she appeared to be older in the picture, Dee Atherton/Bedelia Bisset was a dead ringer for the young woman she'd shot—the woman who now lay in a coma at St. Vincent's.

12

AN HOUR AND A HALF LATER, Gabe drove through the gates of Thorne Mansion just in time for Nicola's fitting with Randolph Meyer. They'd spent most of the drive back to the city trying to process the information that Bedelia Bisset/Dee Atherton and Claire Forlani had to be related. That certainly would explain why they looked so much alike and why the younger woman had been wearing the older woman's bracelet. He'd already texted Jonah to start looking for a connection between Dee Atherton and an Italian in Venice, perhaps named Forlani.

The difference in age along with the resemblance and the bracelet argued that they were mother and daughter. Nicola had pointed out that they couldn't discount aunt and niece.

The call from her stepmother to remind her again of the fitting appointment for her dress had come just as they'd left The Eyrie. Nicola had been in the middle of making an excuse when she'd broken off, listened for a minute and then said, "Fine. We'll be there."

Her voice had been smooth, but he'd noted that her knuckles had turned white on the cell as she replaced it in her purse. Then she'd told him that her father was at the house and wanted to talk to him. She'd been frowning ever since.

"I take it that you aren't happy about the fitting," he said as he parked the truck in front of the sprawling front porch.

"I don't need another fitting. I just had one with Randolph last week. The dress is fine."

Turning in the seat, he took her hand and raised it to his lips. "It's more than the fitting. Tell me."

There was a mix of anger and hurt in her eyes when they met his. "It's the whole dichotomy between what I want to be and what they want me to be. Marcia wants me to marry well, step into her shoes one day, and throw charity balls. So does my father. That's not what I want—or at least not all that I want."

"And this dress-fitting thing symbolizes that?"

Her laugh was dry and lacking in humor. "You might say that. I've had four fittings for this dress because Marcia thinks that Randolph Meyer is just the kind of young man I ought to be seeing socially. Oh, he may not come from money, but he's definitely making his mark here in Denver. And he's invited to all the right parties. In fact, Marcia told me earlier today that he will be joining our table at the ball tomorrow night."

"She's matchmaking." He noted a bitter, coppery taste in his mouth. Jealousy?

"Yes. If I marry someone local, then I'll stay here in Denver. In fact, if your friend Nash Fortune wasn't always flying hither and yon for the air force, I'm sure Marcia would get it into her head that we were soul mates. She already invited him for dinner once she learned that he was stationed at the Air Force Academy, and he'll be sitting at our table tomorrow night, too."

Gabe had arranged for Nash to come in for the ball.

The fact that he was stationed at the Air Force Academy in Colorado Springs made it easy. Gabe was depending on his old friend to help out with security. Jonah was still tying up some business so that he could get away.

"You and Nash," he mused. "I guess I'll just count my lucky stars that my friend puts a high value on serving our country." There had been sufficient annoyance in her tone when she'd spoken of the Meyer guy and Nash to ease the jealousy he was feeling. "But the matchmaking isn't all that's bothering you. Spill it, Curls."

She took a breath and let it out. "Marcia said that my father's there and wants to meet with you. While I'm having this totally unnecessary fitting appointment with Randolph, you and my father will be in his office sharing information on what you and he have discovered so far. I'll be left on the outside just as I was this morning."

He studied her for a moment. "If you don't like what's going to happen in there, change it."

She blinked at him.

He shrugged. "They both love you, Nicola. And you love them. You're smart. You know what they want. That's partly why you accepted the transfer to your father's office after you finished your training. Have you tried telling them exactly what *you* want?"

Nicola opened her mouth and then shut it. She thought of that this very morning when she'd wanted to burst in on the meeting her father was having with Gabe and demand that he include her. But she hadn't. She didn't like to make waves. Temper tantrums had never been her style. She'd always tried to just forge ahead and prove herself by her actions. But maybe there was a middle road.

"Okay." She nodded at Gabe. "Okay."

"That's my Curls." He leaned in for a quick, hard kiss. As if someone had pressed the dimmer button on a stage light, everything around Nicola faded. Fire leapt along her nerve endings. Pleasure swirled through her body. And suddenly, she was drowning in him, sinking down to a place where the air was so thick, she couldn't breathe. Didn't want to.

Even as a nagging little voice told her to pull back, she framed his face with her hands and absorbed the sharp angle of his cheekbones, the strength of his jaw. She heard a sound, but she couldn't make it out over the thundering of her heart.

In what dull, little-used corner of his mind had he thought he could make the kiss a quick one? Not happening—not while she could make lights explode in his head and heat swarm his system. He scraped his teeth along her lower lip, absorbing the softness and the ripe taste of her surrender. Maybe it was that particularly addictive flavor that had him coming back for more and not being able to pull away. Or maybe it was just *her*.

She made a sound in her throat that vibrated through him. He wanted to hear it again. Had to hear it again. Lord, he wanted to touch her. But he knew that if he did, he wouldn't be able to stop. Why had he parked smack in front of the house? If he'd just pulled over a little farther back down the drive, he could have—would have—

He pushed the button on her seat belt and was about to grip her shoulders and pull her across the console when she lifted her hands and gave him a shove—as hard as a couple of the blocks she'd thrown on the basketball court.

It took a second for his brain cells to click on, another for him to pull in a breath. For a moment neither of them said a word. It gave him some satisfaction that her eyes were as blurry as he suspected his own were.

"That's the one bad thing about this pickup. No backseat."

She drew in a shaky breath and inched just a little farther away from him. "It's the parking location that's really bad. I have a feeling that the front seat would have proved more than adequate if I couldn't feel Marcia's eyes on me."

Gabe glanced up at the windows, and he saw one of the curtains twitch. "I'll be damned."

"No." She sighed. "But I probably will be."

"Good call, Curls. How did you know?"

Her tone went dry. "I grew up here. Every time a date drove me home, Marcia was on duty at that very window."

He grinned at her as he gripped her chin. "Ready to face the music?"

"Yes. Yes, I am."

THERE WERE THREE PEOPLE waiting to greet them as Nicola strolled into the foyer of Thorne Mansion with Gabe just a step behind her. Nicola's father and stepmother were joined by Randolph Meyer. Marcia came forward first to embrace her in a hug.

"Anna is waiting in your old room to help you change into the dress."

"In a minute." Out of the corner of her eye, she caught her father signaling Gabe to follow him.

"Dad?"

Her father turned to her.

"Before I do the dress fitting thing, Gabe and I need to talk to you, and I'd like to see the security setup for tomorrow night."

"But Randolph's on a schedule," Marcia protested.

"It's fine," Randolph said. "I'm more than happy to wait."

"Thanks." Nicola shot him a smile before she and Gabe

followed her father up the staircase and along the hall that led to Thorne Mansion's Grand Salon.

Her father pressed numbers into a pad on the door.

"How many people have access to the code?" Nicola asked.

"Gabe, his assistant Debra Bancroft, your stepmother and I have the code. Yesterday, G. W. Securities added a thumbprint to the access protocol. Marcia's, mine and Gabe's. Debra saw to the installation as part of the walk-through."

Nick turned to Gabe. "Marcia said that Debra stopped by earlier just to check on everything again."

"That sounds like Debra," Gabe said. "I've given her a lot of responsibility for this job."

Nicola studied Gabe, but she couldn't read anything in his expression. "Thumbprints can be lifted."

He nodded as they stepped into the salon. "My father once told me that there isn't a security system in the world that can't be breached—given the time. That's why the thumbprint was added yesterday. Working around it may slow the thief down a bit."

"Only slow him down?" Nicola asked.

"As you said, thumbprints can be lifted, and if I were the thief, I'd assume that your stepmother would have access. I'd come with her thumbprint and perhaps your father's. But only if I intended to enter through this door."

Together they entered the room. It was long and narrow. Late-afternoon sunlight slanted through the windows and glinted off honey-toned parquet floors. As far as Nicola knew, the salon was only used for the Valentine's Day charity auction each year. It was sparsely furnished to allow a maximum number of guests. Cocktails would be served here from 6:00 to 8:00 to allow time for guests to view the Cézanne and place their bids. Then everyone would exit to the upstairs ballroom for dinner and dancing. Marcia would announce the painting's new owner at midnight.

The Cézanne hung on a wall directly across from the access door. It was completely enclosed in glass, and there was another keypad with a thumbprint component. Next to it was a small green light.

"The glass is shatterproof," Gabe said.

"But the keypad looks the same as the one on the door," Nicola commented. "With the code and the proper thumbprint, this shouldn't take the thief long."

"I agree."

"They still have to get out," Nick Guthrie said. "We'll have men on the room."

"He or she won't use the door to exit," Gabe said. "This house is a historic landmark. The blueprints are on file. Any thief worth his salt will know how to get in and out without using the door. And to maximize time, they'll create a distraction in another part of the house to deflect attention from this room."

"Are you saying that the thief will get away with stealing this painting?" Guthrie asked.

Gabe smiled. "No, I'm merely saying that at some time tomorrow night, the thief will stand this close to the painting—and he or she will believe they're home free."

Nicola narrowed her eyes on the keypad again. Then she pointed to the green light. "The access code and the thumbprint won't be enough. You've installed the same new security system on this that you installed on the statue of St. Francis."

"You've got good eyes, Curls."

"Well, I'll be damned." Nick Guthrie bent close to inspect the light. "When did you install that?"

"Last week shortly after the keypad was installed."

"You weren't here last week. I've had men watching

the house since the painting arrived and we authenticated it. None of our alarm systems have been breached. I've personally checked the painting each day."

"What kind of a security expert would I be if I couldn't get past my own systems?"

Nicola smiled at the perplexed expression on her father's face. "That's exactly why Gabe was my prime suspect."

"How would you get the painting out if you were the thief?" Guthrie had postponed asking that question until he'd escorted them into the room he used as his home office and gestured them into chairs. Gabe figured by that time, he'd had a chance to mull over what he'd just learned.

"I'd come in the way I actually did—through an old heating air duct—after I bypassed the alarm system on the house," Gabe said. "I considered using one of the windows, but that would have required more time."

Guthrie narrowed his eyes. "I didn't know you were a second-story expert."

Gabe merely shrugged. "In my business I need to be. And I've had since New Year's Eve to try to get into the mind of the thief. The problem is—the person they're relying on to get through all the security is not going to be with them tomorrow night. So they'll have to improvise. That's why I'm thinking they'll definitely need to create some kind of a distraction."

"You don't think they'll call the whole thing off."

"No. Nicola has discovered some interesting information about the Cézanne." He turned to her. "Why don't you update your father?"

She met her father's eyes. "I was right when I told you that Gabe was at the center of this. No, he's not the thief. But he or his father or both probably are the motivating factor in why these thefts are taking place now."

Gabe leaned back in his chair and listened to as neat and concise a report on a case as he'd ever heard. Starting with the young woman who'd approached his father nearly twenty-five years ago in Paris, she wove a narrative including the attempted theft of the Cézanne collection sixteen years ago and ending with the theft they were expecting to happen the following night.

They'd discussed how the dots might connect on their drive back from seeing his uncle, but hearing it told in chronological order helped Gabe to see it all more clearly.

When she finished, she opened her purse and placed the sketch of the young woman they thought to be Claire Forlani on her father's desk; they added the printout of the driver's license. Gabe brought up the photo of Dee Atherton that Jonah had sent him on his cell.

Guthrie studied them for a moment. "The resemblance is compelling."

"I have my friend Jonah tracing the younger one. He's looking for a birth certificate that somehow connects to the Italian Uncle Ben believes partnered with Dee Atherton in Venice. The dates would be right, and we might have a connection. At this point I have a young man I trust guarding Claire Forlani's room at the hospital. He has orders to call me with updates on her condition and with any news about visitors. If she wakes up, we'll pay her a visit. I haven't informed the hospital of her identity. At this point, I'm not sharing anything I don't have to with my employees or anyone else."

Guthrie nodded. "I don't want anyone in my office working on it, either."

Guthrie included both of them in his glance. "So the two of you think that the Cézanne being auctioned tomorrow night may have been the object all along?"

"Stealing the Cézanne is part of the object," Nicola said. "Framing Gabe for stealing it is also a goal."

Guthrie shifted his gaze to Gabe. "They're trying to get revenge because your father didn't help this Dee Atherton-slash-Bedelia Bisset steal a painting from the Robineaus' Cézanne collection, and as a result, she was killed while she was trying to do it with her partner. I can perhaps buy into that. But why didn't they just get revenge on your father? Why are they trying to frame you for these new thefts?"

"Because Gabe was a major reason why his father wouldn't help in that original robbery. Raphael Wilder came home to raise his son. He made a promise to Gabe's mother that he was out of the business. They could believe Gabe shares in the blame for Dee Atherton's death."

Guthrie shifted his gaze to the photos again, tapping his fingers on the desk. "I still don't understand why they didn't just get revenge at the time—on your father."

"Maybe they did," Nicola said.

They both turned to look at her. "Maybe they got revenge on him by framing him for the theft of the Matisse."

Guthrie frowned. "Raphael Wilder stole that painting."

"He never confessed," Nicola pointed out.

"The jails are filled with people who claim to be innocent."

When he rose and strode to the window, Nicola followed. "If you step back and look at the whole picture, you have to admit it makes sense."

He turned to face her. "Then why didn't Raphael Wilder just tell me?"

There were several beats of silence while they thought about that. Gabe studied the two of them standing toe to toe, frowning at each other. They were very much alike.

Finally, he said, "Maybe my father didn't know who was framing him. If you think about it, the whole plan hinged on him not knowing. That way he had no way to defend himself."

"Pretty perfect," Nicola mused. "And cold. And that coldness is exactly what it would take to wait this long to get revenge on Gabe."

Guthrie ran a hand through his hair. But he kept his eyes on Nicola. Gabe could tell his old friend still wasn't buying it, not totally.

"Okay." Nicola waved a hand. "Take my theory about the Matisse being a part of this off the table for now. Let's just concentrate on what we know for sure. Dee Atherton comes to Raphael Wilder for help or advice on her upcoming job to rob the Denver Art Museum. He refuses to help, and she's killed. Her partner gets away."

"And he waits sixteen years to get revenge on Gabe?" Guthrie asked. "Why? And don't just give me that stuff about revenge being a dish best served cold."

For a moment, Nicola merely continued to frown, considering the question. Gabe waited for her to think it through and knew the instant she had it.

"Couple of reasons. Sixteen years ago, Gabe was just a kid. There's more to take away, more to destroy now. And Dee Atherton's partner was a forger. Dee was the one who could disable security systems." She glanced from Gabe to her father. "Perhaps the thief discovered at some point that Claire Forlani had inherited Dee's talents and then had to wait for her to grow up in order to fully take revenge. He may even have kept in contact with Claire over the years."

"I'll have Jonah check into that," Gabe said.

"Dammit," Guthrie said. "You're beginning to make sense." He turned to Gabe. "We need to find out who Dee

Atherton's partner was. I'll call Interpol, see if I can find out anything through channels."

Guthrie returned to his desk and sat down. Then he gestured Nicola back into her chair. "I've got something to report although it isn't nearly as dramatic. A statue of St. Francis was one of the artifacts that the FBI confiscated from your mother's art studio when we executed the original search warrant. It was signed out earlier this week a day after the article on the statue ran in the Sunday magazine section."

"By whom?"

"The name on the sign-out sheet was Mary Thomas. The clerk described a woman who might be Mary and swears she presented Mary's I.D. The signature was in Mary's handwriting. I checked the sign-out sheet myself. She wasn't in the office at the time."

"Have you spoken with her about it?" Gabe asked.

"No. If she's involved in this, I don't want to give her any warning until we have proof. You've already rattled their cages."

"And it isn't proof. We already know that one member of the team is a good forger," Nicola pointed out.

"Or Mary could have lent her I.D. to someone who was her height and weight," Gabe said.

"But the fact that the statue was signed out just before the attempt on the St. Francis," Nicola said, "supports my idea that framing Gabe is a big part of this."

"It would also mean that there's someone involved who would know or have access to a list of what was taken in that original search. That's likely to be someone in my office," Guthrie said. "If not Mary, then someone else."

Gabe didn't argue with him. Neither did Nicola.

Guthrie's frown deepened. "I didn't head up the investigation of the attempt at the Denver museum, but I do know that this Bedelia Bisset-slash-Dee Atherton's partner got away clean. There wasn't even a whiff of who he was. It was a couple of rookies who arrived first on the scene and neither one of them got the license plate of the van. I'll access the files first thing in the morning. Discreetly."

"There's another wrinkle in this that we ought to tell you about," Gabe said. "In addition to the strong possibility that this group might include someone working for you or me, Nicola thinks that they may have someone with access to Denver's very elite social circle feeding them information."

Guthrie thought for a moment. "It makes sense." He rose then, paced to the window. "We're making progress, but I don't like it. I don't like it at all."

"Why not?" Nicola asked.

He turned back to face them. "If you're right and revenge is a key element, and this elaborate plot was triggered by the death of Dee Atherton, aka Bedelia Bisset, then history is repeating itself in a way."

"What do you mean?" Nicola asked.

"Sixteen years ago, a woman was shot and killed during a failed attempt to steal the Cézanne collection," Nick Guthrie said. "Yesterday, you shot a young woman we believe is involved in planning and executing another attempt to steal one of those same Cézannes and she's currently in an intensive care unit."

Nicola swallowed hard. "If Claire Forlani doesn't pull through, then she, too, will have been fatally injured in a failed robbery."

"Exactly," Guthrie said. "If she's related to Dee Atherton and you're right about the fact that the mastermind behind this is hell-bent on punishing Gabe, then stealing the Cézanne tomorrow night may take second place to revenge. Both of you may be in mortal danger."

"THE DRESS IS PERFECT," Marcia said. "And it's so right for Valentine's Day. Randolph has such a good eye. Red is your color. Turn around so that you can see it from all angles."

Red, schmed. But Nicola didn't say the words out loud. The last place she wanted to be was closeted with Marcia in her room trying on a dress. She wanted to be with her father and Gabe so that they could bounce more ideas off one another. Her mind was spinning with possibilities. The whole series of thefts was beginning to remind her of an onion. Each time they peeled back a layer, there was more.

How much more? That was what they had to find out.

"Of course, you'll have to fix your hair. Smooth it back or better still, just let your curls frame your face."

Nicola bit down on her lower lip. Discussing her hair-style was not going to get her downstairs any sooner. At least when Marcia had entered the library to drag her away, she'd first shooed the two men into the salon to share tea with Randolph Meyer. Her gut told her that her father's analysis was dead-on. Guarding the Cézanne wasn't the only problem they would have at the charity ball tomorrow night.

And that meant that the sooner they could get a handle on who they were dealing with, the better. "Randolph designs for a lot of your friends, doesn't he?"

"I've been recommending him to everyone. I like to do that when I see a young person who needs a helping hand. But I can't take full credit for the way he's caught on. I recommended him to Betsy Langford last summer, and she passed his name on to as many people as I have. Maybe more. She's very close friends with the Glastons. Randolph's designing several dresses for the ball, including Mariah Bailey's, and she only shops in New York or L.A.

But Randolph is catching on with everyone. Mary Thomas has been a fan of his for quite some time. And this afternoon when Debra Bancroft stopped by, she and Randolph discussed some of the changes he's made for her dress for the ball. She's working security, but she has to blend in."

Nicola felt her pulse actually skip a beat. Randolph had been in every single house the thieves had hit or intended to hit. Plus, he'd designed dresses for two of the people who were on the possible suspect list. She needed to talk to Gabe. "You're right, Marcia. The dress *is* perfect." She turned back to face the mirror. "Can you help me with the zipper?"

"You haven't even looked at it," Marcia said. "And Randolph will want to see it on you before he leaves. That was why he delivered it in person."

Biting back an inward sigh, Nicola faced the mirror again. And since she would have to fake it anyway, she really did look at the dress. It was the simplicity of the sketch Randolph had shown her that had appealed to her from the beginning. There was no doubt in her mind that he was a talented designer. From narrow straps at her shoulders, the material angled to a V neckline, then flowed smoothly along the lines of her body, stopping just above her knees.

"He's shortened it since the last fitting," she noted with a frown.

Marcia waved a hand. "That's because he noticed your legs. The benefit of working with a designer is that he tailors the clothes to your strengths."

Nicola gave the dress a second sweep with her gaze. As a child, Marcia had dressed her in ruffles and ribbons and pink had been her signature color. Probably as a result of that, Nicola tended to favor conservative tailoring and colors in her work wardrobe, and slacks were more practical than skirts.

While the dress couldn't be called flashy, it went a few steps beyond conservative. In her mind, she'd pictured it in black. Randolph was the one who'd decided that red would suit her better. And she supposed it did. Turning, she angled her head just enough to see that the hemline wasn't the only thing the designer had altered. He'd definitely lowered the back and taken in a couple of seams. It was a far cry from the party or prom dresses of her younger years.

And it made her think of Gabe. She definitely didn't look like an FBI agent in the dress. And she didn't feel like one either. She felt like a woman.

And the giddy idea of wanting Gabe to see her in a sexy red dress was the last thing she should be thinking about.

"I have a confession to make," Marcia said.

At her tone, Nicola turned to face her and was surprised at the sheepish expression on her stepmother's face. "What is it?"

"When I invited Randolph to sit at our table tomorrow night, I was hoping that you and he would hit it off. He seems so right for you. He loves art, you know. Last night, he couldn't stop talking about the Cézanne. He went to college with Celia Robineau, so he's familiar with the painting. I was so sure that you and he would hit it off."

Nicola smiled wryly as she took her stepmother's hands in hers. "I know why you invited Randolph to sit with us. You invited Nash Fortune to dinner for the same reason. You want to match me up with someone."

"It's that obvious?"

Nicola leaned in to give her stepmother a quick kiss on her cheek. Then she thought of Gabe's advice. "What's obvious is that you want me to be happy. I am. And I will be. It just may not be your vision of how I should be happy."

"But I never once thought of Gabe. I should have."

Nicola stared at her stepmother. "Gabe and I are working together on these robberies. We aren't..." What exactly weren't they? "It's not what you think...we're not..."

Taking her hand, Marcia drew her toward the door. "Nicola, I saw the way the two of you were kissing in the truck. You're definitely on to something. Your father has always had a special fondness for that boy. How long have you been seeing each other?"

"We haven't. I mean..." Less than twenty-four hours if she didn't count those Saturdays on the basketball court at the St. Francis Center.

Marcia patted her hand. "I was the same way when I first met your father. I couldn't seem to catch enough breath to get a complete sentence out. You'll get used to it."

No, Nicola thought as Marcia steered her out of the room. She was pretty sure that she wasn't going to ever get used to it. She didn't even know what "it" was.

13

WHEN NICOLA ENTERED the salon with her stepmother, Gabe completely lost his train of thought. Tea sloshed over the rim of his cup onto his saucer. She was stunning. Had he ever thought of her as beautiful before? Attractive—very. Sexy—definitely. But in the red dress, she was breathtaking. It was simple, but it clung to every curve as if it had been designed specifically with her in mind.

And, of course it had been. Perhaps it was the lingering trace of jealousy that had his brain cells clicking on again. In any case it helped to shift his gaze from Nicola to the tall blond man with the athletic body and Hollywood handsome features. Randolph Meyer had taken Nicola's hand the instant she'd entered and he'd drawn the two women to the far end of the salon where a circle of bay windows let in the late-afternoon sunlight. The three of them were oohing and ahhing over the dress as if it were a work of art.

For Gabe it was the woman who made the dress and not the other way around.

"What exactly is your relationship with my daughter?"

Gabe spilled more tea. The question was not only unexpected, it made his stomach lurch.

Nick Guthrie took the cup from his hand and placed it on a nearby table.

"She and I are…" What? Lovers? That was a hell of a thing to tell her father. And wasn't this a big part of why he'd avoided Nicola for three long months?

"We're—" he began again and got no further. Seeing each other? Dating? Neither of those descriptions quite fit.

"I saw you kissing her in the truck when you drove up. All of us did."

"All?" Gabe turned to look at Guthrie then.

"Randolph, Marcia and I. We were all in the window when you drove up. The curtains are sheer."

"Sorry. I forgot where we were."

Guthrie set his own tea down. "How long have we worked together?"

Wary of the shift in topic, Gabe studied the older man. Then he said, "You called me in the first time to consult on a case six years ago. A safe deposit box that you wanted opened and you didn't want to destroy the evidence you expected to find inside."

Guthrie nodded. "See, you remembered that all right. In fact, I've never known you to forget anything. I'm going to try again. What is your relationship with my daughter?"

Gabe shifted his gaze to Nicola, then back to her father. "I'm trying to figure it out."

Guthrie studied him for a moment and for some reason Gabe couldn't fathom, he seemed satisfied with the answer. "The problem is, until you do figure it out, it's distracting you."

Gabe couldn't argue with that.

"Will it interfere with your keeping her safe?"

"No. I'll keep her safe." He kept his eyes steady on Guthrie's. "And I'll have help on that score. She's smart. We wouldn't have as much as we have right now if it weren't for her. And she's pretty good at keeping herself safe."

Guthrie glanced at Nicola and then back at Gabe. "I'll have to put my trust in both of you then."

The two women and Randolph Meyer chose that moment to start toward them. Guthrie spoke in a voice only Gabe could hear. "When this is over, I'm going to ask my question again. You'd better have it figured out by then."

BECAUSE IT WAS MUCH EASIER to think about the case than the look she'd seen in Gabe's eyes when she'd modeled the red dress, or the unsettling conversation she'd had with her stepmother, the moment that they'd made their escape from Thorne Mansion, Nicola filled Gabe in on what she'd learned about Randolph Meyer. "If Mary Thomas or Debra Bancroft are involved in these thefts, he could have provided very useful information to them."

"But you don't think he's the mastermind."

"Too young. I think that the person behind all of this has to be Dee Atherton's old partner—someone Dee might have told about your mother's studio and who might even have seen that statue of St. Francis you and your father worked on."

"Not a bad thought, Curls. If my memory is correct, we were working on that statue during the time when Dee visited my father."

"I think we ought to pay Father Mike a visit."

At Gabe's questioning glance, she said, "You said that one of the places you and your father spent time during that summer was at the St. Francis Center. You met Jonah and Nash and played with them while your father sat in the garden talking to Father Mike."

"And you're interested in what they might have talked about."

"Yes. He might have confided in a priest, things that he might not have told even your Uncle Ben."

Gabe dialed a number, pinned down the location of the priest, and twenty minutes later they knocked on the front door of the Franciscan monastery where Father Mike now lived. It was a huge building, Gothic in design.

"How much do you trust Father Mike?" she asked while they waited.

"He'd be right in there with Jonah and Nash, your father and you. Just what are you going to ask him?"

"Not sure yet. Just checking my parameters."

"You have none," Gabe said.

The door opened then and Father Mike beamed a smile at them, then led the way into a library.

The priest gestured them onto a sofa and took one of the chairs facing them. In front of him on a low table sat a crystal decanter and three glasses. "Would you care for some sherry? If you say yes, then I won't feel guilty about having one myself."

"Then yes," Nicola said. "It's been a long day."

When he'd poured the wine and handed out the glasses, he sat back in his chair and sipped. "You said you had some questions?"

Gabe gave her an *after you* gesture.

"The summer before Raphael Wilder was arrested, he brought Gabe to the center to play basketball with Jonah and Nash. And he spent time with you talking. We'd like to ask about those conversations if we could. If they're not protected by the seal of confession?"

Father Mike smiled at her. "Raphael wasn't Catholic. So I was never his priest in that sense. What would you like to know?"

"Do you know why he decided to sculpt a statue of St. Francis in marble?" Nicola asked.

Surprise and pleasure lit the priest's features. "I didn't know that he had. Was it a good likeness?"

"Nearly perfect," she said.

"He let me help him work on it." Gabe sipped his sherry before setting the glass on the table.

"I did know that he had decided to try his talent at sculpting," Father Mike said. "Your mother had suggested it. He was a talented painter, and she wanted him to find a new challenge. She was concerned that Denver might become a bit boring."

"Was he worried about that, too?" Gabe asked.

"A little. But your father was a resilient man. He loved you and your mother very much. If he had regrets about leaving his old way of life, it was that he hadn't left it sooner. I'd love to see the statue."

"I can arrange that," Gabe said.

Nicola studied the two men as Gabe went on to explain where they'd found the statue and that this wasn't the first time the thief had left a forgery in place of the art he'd stolen.

"Leaving a forgery behind—your mother told me that was what your father had always done," Father Mike said.

Nicola reached out and took Gabe's hand. "If the thief had succeeded last night in making the switch, I think Gabe would be in jail right now. Did he ever mention a woman named Dee Atherton or Bedelia Bisset?"

Father Mike frowned thoughtfully. "You're talking about that woman who was killed during the attempted robbery on the Denver Art museum. Your father called her Dee. She was the original reason why Raphael sought me out. He felt guilty about her death. He said he'd worked with her before, and she'd come to him twice here in Denver to ask for advice."

Father Mike set his glass on the table. "He refused both times and explained why he couldn't because of promises he'd made. He told her not to come again."

"He felt guilty because he hadn't helped her?" Gabe asked.

"Yes. She'd put him in a difficult position. If he'd helped her, he'd have broken a vow he'd made to your mother. But afterward, he couldn't help thinking that if he'd listened and given her advice, she might not have died. And, of course, the guilt only grew when he received the note."

"The note?" Gabe asked.

Father Mike nodded. "He received a threatening note a week after the woman was shot. It said, *You're to blame. You'll pay.* When he showed it to me, I told him to give it to the police."

"He didn't?" Nicola felt Gabe's hand fist beneath hers.

Father Mike shook his head. "He refused. They'd already questioned him about the attempt on the museum. He figured that if he showed them the note, there wasn't much chance they'd take it seriously. They might even take a harder look at him. He didn't have much use for the police. Then nothing happened."

"Until the Matisse was discovered in Gabe's mother's studio," Nicola said.

Father Mike narrowed his eyes. "You think that's connected to Dee Atherton's death?"

"She does," Gabe said. "And she's beginning to convince me she might be right."

"Interesting." Father Mike said nothing for a moment as he sipped his sherry. "St. Francis works in mysterious ways."

"How so?" Nicola prompted.

But it was Gabe he looked at when he spoke. "The real reason your father first brought you to the center was so that he could say a prayer to St. Francis. Your mother had told him about the statue's power. His prayer was that he wouldn't fail you or her. I've never believed that he did."

"WE'LL HEAD TO YOUR place next," Gabe said as he drove the truck away from the monastery. "You can pack what you need." He shot her a glance. "I promised your father that I would protect you, and my place has better security."

"I can hardly argue with that. My apartment isn't far. Take a right at the next light."

After making the turn, Gabe said, "Thanks."

"For what?"

"You did a great job of questioning Father Mike. I'd never thought to ask those questions before."

"You weren't so bad yourself."

He shot her a glance. "Looking back, I can see my faith in my father was mostly denial. I didn't want to look too closely at what had led to his arrest because I was probably afraid of the answers."

"You were the one who said he was framed. You're the one who started me thinking how that fact might shift the perspective on everything about this case."

"But I didn't pursue trying to prove his innocence at the time. Or since."

"You were thirteen. You'd lost your mother, but you had your father. A man who'd promised to stay with you, a man who'd only shared holidays with you so far. Then two months after he was sentenced, he was taken away also. And you're beating up on yourself because you didn't turn into a supersleuth and clear your dad? Instead, you kept your promise to him. You built a career, a life where you stop people from doing what he did."

The passion in her voice had something inside of Gabe easing. She had an ability to do that for him—to smooth away hurts that he hadn't even known were there.

"For what it's worth, the whole time that I was compiling research on this case, I never once questioned your father's guilt. Planting that Matisse was a perfect plan. And very cold. Most people who want revenge need for the victim of it to know. This person evidently doesn't need that. And he or she may just get away with it again."

"We're not going to let that happen."

They drove in silence for a few minutes. Then Nicola said, "Father Mike thinks the prayer-granting power of the statue is playing a key role in all of this."

"Yeah, I got that. I've certainly prayed to St. Francis a few times. And I have to admit I was hoping last night that the power of the statue would help me trap the thief."

"Take the next left," she directed. "Did you ever say a prayer to it back when you were at the center?"

"Sure. Father Mike made Jonah, Nash and me all say a prayer. It was the traditional prayer to St. Francis, the *Lord, Make Me an Instrument of Your Peace* prayer.

"Where there is darkness, let me sow light, where there is doubt, faith—is that the one?"

Gabe nodded. "But at the end he told us to add one more petition. He even told us what to pray for."

"What?"

"That we would find what we were supposed to find in life. Pretty general and pretty hard to figure out when or if he would answer it. I thought he had once I'd established G. W. Securities."

"And you don't think so now?"

He shrugged. "Lately, I've been…restless…thinking that there's something more."

"You could always give sculpting another whirl."

"Right. I'm pretty sure that's not the direction St. Francis is pushing me in." He glanced at her. "How about you? Did you ever say a prayer to the statue?"

"A couple."

"Have they come true?"

She turned to study him, recalling that long ago prayer she said when she was ten. "The last day I played basketball with you and my stepmother found out that's what I'd been doing, I prayed to St. Francis that I would see you again. I didn't think he'd answered me. But I guess he has."

"Father Mike used to tell us that prayers aren't always answered the way you expect them to be."

Nicola smiled. "There's a news bulletin. Oh, turn left on this next street. I live in the third building down on the right."

Gabe slowed in front of an old brick building, a renovated factory. Shops and restaurants were sprinkled along the street.

"I park in there." She pointed to a lot across the street and handed him her card to swipe.

"An underground garage would be safer," he said as he pulled into an empty slot.

"Then I'd be in an enclosed space. Here there are lights, traffic, a good chance of people strolling by. If I screamed, someone would hear me."

He got out of the truck and circled around to open her door.

"Besides, I have a doorman. Charlie keeps a pretty good eye on all of his residents." As they crossed the street, she pointed to the man standing behind glass doors and waving at her.

"You've given this speech before," he guessed.

"To both my mother and my father. Hi, Charlie," she said as they stepped into the building. "This is Gabe."

Charlie had a portly build and a friendly smile, but his gaze turned speculative when he looked at Gabe. "You'd be the one who sent the flowers? I sent the delivery man up and told him to leave them outside the door."

"Flowers?" They said the word in unison.

Charlie nodded. "For Valentine's Day. You have no idea how many deliveries there have been today. I couldn't keep up with all of them. When this guy came in with three huge vases, he asked if he could help out by taking them up. I checked the logo on the cards, and when I saw he was from the flower shop down the street, I sent him up. You'll find them right outside your door."

"Thanks, Charlie," Nicola said as she and Gabe stepped into the elevator. The instant the doors slid shut all the way, she pulled her gun out.

"Maybe they're from Randolph Meyer," Gabe said.

"Maybe."

"But you're not banking on it."

"I have a suspicious mind."

"I like the way it works." Gabe waited until the doors slid open again before he took his weapon out.

"You're armed," she noted in a barely audible voice.

"I run a security firm." He held up a hand and she listened with him. The muted rumble of a TV drifted from the far end of the hall. Otherwise, there was nothing. And there was no bouquet of flowers sitting in front of any door.

"Which one is yours?" Gabe whispered.

But she didn't have to give him an answer. The first one on their right was ajar. He moved to the far side; she took the near.

"Ready?" she mouthed.

At his nod, she booted the door open. He went in high, she low. Even as she scanned the debris, she knew there was no one there. Still she kept her gun raised, and Gabe covered her back as they checked the rest of the place out. She felt the rage and tamped down on it. Rage wasn't what she needed now.

The destruction had been thorough but selective. Nicola made a mental list of the damage as they moved through the rooms. It helped her focus. Her sofa had been slashed from end to end. So had the drapes.

And there in the middle of her coffee table was a huge arrangement of red roses and white lilies in a vase. Together, they moved past it to the kitchen. Her cereal and coffee grounds were scattered across the floor. Eggs had been tossed into the mix along with the contents of two bottles of soft drink and a wilted bunch of broccoli.

"Good thing I only keep the basics here," she said.

"Broccoli is basic?"

The question had some of the rage inside of her easing. "It fits into one of the essential food groups. I keep one in the fridge as a reminder."

"Ah."

It didn't escape her attention that he'd moved slightly in front of her since they'd entered, nor that he remained in that position and shielded her from the windows as they made their way to the bedroom. But there was no one here. Whoever had destroyed her apartment was long gone.

Her heart sank the moment she stepped around him to get a good look at her bed. She'd brought home a gallon of paint, intending to replace the bright yellow on the walls. The blue color she'd spent time selecting now decorated her mattress and a pile of clothes that had been pulled off hangers.

"You can get new clothes," Gabe said.

"Yeah."

He moved to check the bathroom. "Everything seems

fine in here. Nothing broken. He either got tired or ran out of time. Was anything taken?"

"I don't think so." *Nothing broken.* As she repeated the words in her mind, Nicola turned in the doorway and scanned the living room again. Her TV and stereo were fine. Her laptop untouched. No lamps overturned. "He didn't want to make any noise. I live on a street with shops and shoppers. Two or three hours ago, someone outside might have heard something."

"You'll have to add that detail to your spiel about the security here," he said as he joined her. "It definitely saved some of your things."

"Charlie may have been a surprise, too. He would have gotten suspicious if the delivery person had spent more time. And he may have a description. He has good eyes."

"What else do you see, Curls?"

She glanced back at the bedroom, then shifted her gaze back to the sofa. "Anger."

"I agree. Angry people make mistakes. Charlie may be able to describe him."

She allowed her eyes to settle on the flowers again. The arrangement screamed Valentine's Day, as did the large heart that dangled from a red ribbon. Gabe moved with her as she walked to the table. His fingers linked with her free hand when she reached for the heart.

Charlie had been right about the logo of the flower shop down the street. When she turned it over, she found the message card tucked into a pink lace pocket and pulled it out.

You're to blame. You'll pay.

A chill moved through her, but she also felt a tingle. "These are the same words as in the note your father received. This proves there's a connection between what's going on now and Dee Atherton's death."

"And whoever wrote them no longer cares if we put it together," Gabe said. "They want us to."

"Do you think they'll still go after the Cézanne?"

"Absolutely. That was the original goal and my father interfered with it by not participating, then Dee was shot. You've interfered in this one by shooting Claire."

She looked at him then. "You think my father is right—that stealing the Cézanne might not be only their goal anymore."

"I think we're no longer dealing with someone who will wait sixteen years to take their revenge."

14

TWO HOURS LATER, Nicola sat at the gleaming granite counter that framed Gabe's kitchen while he poured a dark red wine into two glasses. She'd had to file a police report, and while she'd answered questions for the two uniforms who'd responded to her initial call, Gabe had filled her father in.

It turned out that Charlie hadn't gotten a very good look at the delivery man's face because of all the flowers. He'd described a tall, lean man wearing black-framed glasses and a cap with a visor and ear flaps. It wasn't much to go on.

Gabe punched buttons on his microwave and set it humming.

"You don't cook at all, do you?" she asked.

He grinned as he set one of the glasses in front of her. "And you do?"

"It takes up time I'd rather spend doing other things."

"Exactly. That's what I always told Uncle Ben when he wanted to teach me." He placed a bowl of French bread on the counter between them. Then he lifted his glass, touched it to hers. "Here's to takeout and microwaves."

"And to state of the art wine coolers." She hadn't missed

the fact that he had one. As a highly trained FBI agent, she knew that people who invested in them tended to have very good taste in wine, and she wasn't disappointed when she sipped hers. The cabernet he'd selected was dark and rich and smooth.

"I forgot something," he murmured, setting his glass down. To her surprise, he located two candles and lit them. Then he moved to a wall and pressed a button. The muted sound of a bluesy sax floated into the room.

At her look, he said, "Just because I don't cook doesn't mean I don't know the elements of fine dining."

She laughed then. And though she couldn't explain it, some of the fear and anger that she'd been tamping down ever since she'd kicked in the door of her apartment eased.

She owed that to Gabe Wilder. He was taking care of her. Not in the hovering way that her parents often had. No, his technique was much more subtle. Back at the apartment, he'd never left her side while she'd called the police and reported the break-in. Earlier, when they'd first stepped out of the elevator on her floor, he hadn't tried to push her aside or go all protective male on her. She liked his style.

She wasn't used to it, but she was sure she could adjust to it. Quite easily.

And why did that scare her? Why did thinking about it tighten the knots in her stomach that had twisted there when she'd talked with her stepmother earlier?

"What is it, Curls?"

He'd reached to cover her hand with his just as the microwave binged. If it hadn't, she just might have told him. She might have simply asked the question. Where were they headed? She'd always known before. Sure, she might have taken some detours to please her parents. But with Gabe the territory was uncharted. Fear bubbled up again.

It wasn't the time to think about that. They needed to focus their attention on the case.

Mental list time. Once they'd caught the thieves and put them away, she'd deal with Gabe. She took another sip of her wine. She simply couldn't think about what she was going to do about him right now.

"I hope you like your chili hot."

"As long as it stops just short of cauterizing my vocal chords."

"You're my kind of girl." He was laughing when he turned back to her, but the moment he saw her, his laughter died. And he simply stared. There she was, sitting at his counter, sipping wine. And what he'd just said was true. As the realization struck him, he nearly dropped one of the bowls. She was exactly his kind of girl. It was that simple.

That terrifying.

He managed to get the chili to the counter and find spoons, napkins. When he sat on the stool across from hers, she met his eyes. There was a question in them, and he was pretty sure it was the same question that was hovering in his. He also saw a trace of fear. And he wanted more than anything to soothe it.

"You've got something on your mind. Why don't you just spill it, Curls?"

She frowned at him. "I wasn't looking for this. For you."

"Same goes," he said.

"And we don't have time for it. We have a thief to catch."

"I agree. But right this minute all we have to do is eat this chili and enjoy our wine."

She studied him for a moment. "Okay." Then she dug in. So did he.

He broke off a chunk of bread and handed it to her. "I'm sorry."

"For what?" She dunked a crust into the chili.

"For what happened to your things. I should have foreseen it."

She set the bread down and studied him. "Are you seriously thinking that you're somehow to blame for what happened at my apartment?"

He shrugged. "I should have put a guard on the place."

"You have two men guarding the St. Francis." She ticked that off on a finger. "Another one looking after Claire Forlani. And you're possibly running short of people who work for you that you can fully trust right now."

He picked her spoon up and handed it to her. "I have friends who don't work for me."

"Yeah." She shook the spoon at him. "One of them is digging up more information on Dee Atherton and Claire while we stuff our faces. And I imagine the air force intrudes on the other one's time."

"Besides Jonah and Nash."

She shook her head. "You have a problem, Wilder."

News bulletin there, he thought as he took another bite of chili.

"You're hung up on taking care of people."

He nearly choked.

"You've arranged things so that Father Mike can work in your Boys and Girls Club for as long as he wants. You've made sure that your Uncle Ben's social life is buzzing right along."

Gabe held up a hand. "Not guilty on that one. He does pretty well on his own."

"I don't doubt it. But besides a bevy of females surrounding him, he still has a poker night with the guys. And that's thanks to you."

"I like playing poker."

"And now you've taken me on. You persuaded my father to put me in the field by convincing him that I needed protection."

Gabe left that one alone. "From what I can see, you take pretty good care of yourself." He lifted his wine and sipped it. "This whole thing started with you saving my life. So in the taking-care-of department, I think we're even. Are you finished with that?"

"No." She dug into her chili again as he took his bowl to the sink and rinsed it.

"I'm right about this. Your whole business, your career is devoted to protecting people and the things they love. I'd say that the prayer you said to St. Francis all those years ago was answered."

He sat down again at the counter and sipped his wine. "Any caregiver genes that I inherited came from my mom. I didn't realize it at the time, but she kept us together as a family. She made it so easy for my father to enter into our life when he came home on holidays. We used to mark off the days on the calendar until the next one. Then he'd arrive a few days ahead of time with presents and plans. We had celebration dinners. After a week or two, he'd leave."

"He came every holiday?"

"All of the major ones. Memorial Day, Fourth of July, Labor Day, Thanksgiving, Christmas. On Valentine's Day he always had a special dinner with my mom to celebrate their wedding anniversary."

She felt a tingle. "I've thought all along that there has to be a reason that this thief only strikes on holidays. There has to be a connection to your father. And he never worked on a holiday because he was always visiting you."

"What are you thinking?"

"The glitch in security in the San Francisco museum

when they thought the Matisse might have been stolen. It was on a holiday weekend, wasn't it?"

He narrowed his eyes. "Easter."

"If that's when the Matisse was stolen, it could very well mean that your father would have had an alibi for that robbery. He would have been with you. It's one more piece of evidence that we can look into."

"We'll do that," he said as he circled around the counter to join her. "But not right now."

He took her hands and lifted them one by one to kiss her palms. "You're not bad in the caregiving department yourself. I wanted fresh eyes on this case. Your eyes. You're helping me to think about things, to see things that I hadn't before."

"It's a two-way street."

"But I also wanted you, Nicola. I had very selfish motives when I convinced your father to assign you to me twenty-four-seven."

He leaned forward and brushed his lips across hers.

"I still want you." *Just you.*

Slipping her hands from his, she looped her arms around his neck. "I want you, too."

Forever? That was the question that hovered in the back of his mind, the question that he hadn't been able to acknowledge earlier.

They had now, he told himself as he took his mouth on a journey along her jaw to the soft skin beneath her ear. Now had always been enough for him. For a long time, it had been all that he had.

"Now," he murmured as he drew back.

"Now." She drew his mouth back to hers. But his lips remained soft and teasing on hers, sampling first one angle and then another. Her mouth offered darker riches, but he took his time. They hadn't had enough time yet, not nearly enough.

When she sighed, he slipped his tongue between her lips and sampled. There was the mellow flavor of the wine, the punch of the chili, and the heady, intoxicating taste of her. Gripping her hips, he lifted her off the stool and she wrapped arms and legs around him.

Heat flared immediately, and with it came the intense desire to lower her to the floor and take her right there. It would be so easy and it would finally ease the ache that was with him constantly now. But he wanted more this time. Tamping down on the need, he broke off the kiss and headed toward the stairs.

"Kiss me again," she murmured.

"First, I want you in my bed."

She nipped at his earlobe. "We haven't needed one yet."

"I need it."

"And I need a kiss."

"Be my guest."

She accepted his invitation, brushing her mouth over his and then tracing the shape of his lips with her tongue. He nearly stumbled when she nipped his bottom lip.

"I forgot I was dealing with an FBI agent."

"I'll try to be more gentle." She ran her tongue along his bottom lip to soothe the hurt, then pressed her mouth fully to his.

He did stumble then, nearly dropping to his knees on the top step of the staircase. He tasted hunger. His? Hers? It was so huge and filled him so completely that he forgot to breathe, forgot he needed to. When he drew back, his heart was pounding, his mind spinning, his vision hazy. He had to check and make sure where the bed was. And it took every ounce of his control to lay her on it and then settle himself at her side.

She reached for him, but he captured her wrists with one of his hands and held them above her head. "We have time, Curls. Let's take it. Do you know how long I've wanted you here in my bed?"

"No."

The moment he felt her wrists relax, he released them to run his fingers through her hair. "Ever since that day I saw you standing there in your office. I pictured you lying here with just the moonlight on your skin. And I thought of touching you."

She said nothing, merely watched him as he traced the curve of her cheek, the line of her jaw. But she began to tremble. And when he brushed a finger over the pulse at her throat it quickened. But he didn't dare kiss her again. Not yet.

"I wanted you naked from that first day." He began with her T-shirt, then her bra. It was plain and white and incredibly arousing. More arousing was the fact that each time his hands made contact with her skin, her breath caught and a new tremor moved through her.

"Your shoulders. So smooth and strong." He ran his hands lightly over them. Then he traced just the tip of his finger along the tops of both breasts. "And your skin is so soft right here."

And then because he simply couldn't help himself, he cupped each breast in his hands. "Just right." This time when she trembled, so did he.

As he fumbled with the clasp of her slacks, she tried to help him, but he brushed her hands away. Then he pleasured them both by drawing her slacks down her legs inch by inch and tracing the path of the flesh he exposed with his mouth. Her flavors, her scents, her textures enticed him, entranced him. And still his hunger for her grew.

He'd told her nothing but the truth. He'd dreamed of having her here in his bed from that very first time their eyes met. But he couldn't have known what the reality would be. There was so much to discover. Slowly, he eased her slacks down her legs, pausing to touch, then taste the newly exposed skin. Her pulse beat at the back of her knees. He lingered there to sample, to exploit. To savor. And her ankles—they were so slender and nearly as fragile as her wrists.

No, he couldn't possibly have imagined what the reality would be, nor what it would do to his system to hear her breath catch and release, catch and release.

How could he have known that in seducing her, she would so thoroughly seduce him?

She was sinking so fast. Her vision had blurred. Far away she could hear music. The sound thrummed quietly in her head as it blended with her sighs and the slowly quickening beat of her blood.

He'd showed her strength before. But this was different. Each brush of his finger, each scrape of his nail and flick of his tongue had her plunging deeper and deeper into a place where the air was too thick to breathe. Nothing had ever been like this. Pleasure had never been so intense. Needs had never been so huge. All she could feel was him. All she knew was him.

And then suddenly, he was gone.

"Gabe?" She opened her eyes and saw that he was getting out of his clothes. She held out a hand. "Come back. I want you. Now."

"First I need to do this." He knelt, straddling her as he stretched her arms out to the sides and linked his fingers with hers. Then he lowered his body to cover hers.

Finally they were flesh to flesh, eye to eye. Her fingers gripped his hard when he made a place for himself between her legs and she wrapped hers around him.

"Mine," she said.

"Mine," he agreed. Forever.

He slipped into her then and it was as if their bodies had never been apart. Though it took all of his control, he kept the rhythm slow. As he spun the moment out, the knowledge settled in his heart that this was where he belonged, where he wanted to be. And when her eyes clouded, when she arched against him and cried out, he was helpless to do anything but follow.

15

COFFEE.

Nicola firmly reminded herself of her goal when she stopped halfway down the circular staircase. She'd borrowed Gabe's robe and wrapped a towel turban-style around her hair. But she was tempted to discard both and go back up to the bathroom and jump Gabe. He was shaving. But he'd distracted her when she was showering, and turnabout was fair play.

Coffee, first. She glanced at her watch—nearly 9:00 a.m. She usually had her first shot of caffeine at 6:00 a.m. And they had a job to do. It was the practical Nicola who descended the rest of the stairs. But it was a different Nicola who did a little dance step on her way to the one-cup coffeemaker she's spotted among the gadgets on Gabe's counter.

As she made the coffee, she caught herself humming. And she *never* hummed. Nor did she begin her days with little dance steps. But she'd never before spent a night like the one she'd spent with Gabe.

A girl had to celebrate some way.

She was about to take her first sip when she caught the movement out of the corner of her eye. Then she nearly dropped her mug as two men stepped out of the elevator and into the room.

For an instant, all three of them froze as if someone had pushed the Pause button.

The only thing that got her heart pumping again was that she recognized one of them. Nash Fortune. It was little wonder that the man had been Marcia's selection as bachelor number one. In addition to a healthy inheritance from his grandmother, he had blond hair, handsome features, and a tall, lean body that looked as good in a uniform as it might have looked on a surfboard.

"Nicola." Nash was the first to move and he smiled as he reached her. "What a pleasure to see you again."

She could have hugged him for pretending not to notice that she was barefoot and wearing Gabe's robe.

"Coffee," the other man said as he dropped two bulging fast food bags on the counter and then circled it to commandeer the second mug that was filling in the small coffeemaker.

He had to be Jonah Stone. It had been fifteen years since she'd seen him, but the eyes were still that bottle-green color, and the dark, rough-edged good looks she'd seen in the boy had come to full fruition in the man.

He turned to smile at her. "Good thing I take this stuff black because Gabe is a real Mother Hubbard when it comes to filling up the larder. I'm Jonah, but the way. And help yourself to the food." He jerked a shoulder at Nash. "I brought plenty because pretty boy here only had girly food on his plane when he picked me up in San Francisco. Caviar, pâté, champagne."

"I don't stock my plane to please you, Jonah," Nash said as he opened one of the bags and began to divide it into four piles. "And you serve plenty of fancy food at your nightclubs."

Nicola took a deep swallow of coffee. "I'll just go up and tell Gabe you're here."

"No need." With one smooth move, Jonah blocked access to the stairs and motioned her toward a stool. "Take a load off. I texted him we were coming."

Nash took the mug from her and replaced it with a breakfast sandwich. "Of course, Jonah also told him that we'd ring and let him know when we arrived. But he has this deep-rooted need to show off, so he had to get through the security system without setting off any alarms."

"You helped," Jonah said as he bit into a french fry. "And I want Gabe to know that I'm still his best student."

Wary but oddly charmed by the two men, Nicola climbed onto a stool and retrieved her coffee.

"So what's up between you and Gabe?" Jonah asked.

Nicola tensed.

Nash sent her a rueful look. "You'll have to forgive Jonah. He's rude. What he's trying to ask is how long have you and Gabe been seeing each other?"

Nicola looked from one man to the other. "Jonah's question is more direct, and you look like two very smart men. I think you've figured out what's up."

They exchanged a look.

"*She's* smart, too," Jonah said.

"Holds her own," Nash added.

Then Jonah took the lead again. "What we're really wondering is what your intentions are."

"My intentions? You…you can't be serious."

"We think of Gabe as family," Nash explained.

"Are you just toying with our friend's affections?" Jonah asked.

"Toying with…" She set her mug down hard enough to slosh coffee. "That's…none of your business."

"Good answer," Nash said to Jonah. "Puts you right in your place."

"She has a bit of a temper, too." Jonah bit into his sandwich. "I can see why Gabe would like that."

Nicola narrowed her eyes. "Why don't you run a background check on me?"

"I already did," Jonah said. "Just as soon as Gabe said the two of you were working together."

She looked from one to the other as she tamped down on her temper. "Look, the two of you didn't like me much fifteen years ago, but if you—"

Nash held up a hand. "It wasn't that we didn't like you."

"It's that you were a *girl*," Jonah finished.

She fisted her hands on her hips. "Well, I'm a woman now."

"Exactly. And Gabe doesn't bring women here. He's very careful," Jonah said. "So naturally, we're curious."

"And rude." But she couldn't fault the way they cared for Gabe.

"She's right," Gabe said as he descended the stairs. "You are rude."

"Uh-oh," Jonah mumbled.

"Busted," Nash said. "You started it. You take the first punch."

"I took the first punch last time," Jonah complained.

"I have plenty of punches to go around," Gabe as he put an arm around Nicola's shoulders.

Both men raised their arms in surrender. "How about if we apologize?" Nash asked with his eyes on Jonah.

"I do," Jonah said turning to Nicola. "Sorry. We just worry about Gabe here."

"I think Gabe here can take care of himself," Nicola said.

Nash laughed then. "I like her." He turned to Nicola. "And I apologize, also. And if Gabe insists on punching us, I'll take it easy on him."

"If I were you, I'd quit while I was ahead," Nicola said.

This time it was Jonah who laughed. Then he held out his hand. "I like you, too. I'm pleased to meet you again, Nicola Guthrie."

She took his hand. "Likewise, I think."

"Pull up a stool," Nash said to Gabe. "Jonah was sure you were starving."

When Gabe had coffee in front of him, he said to Jonah, "You didn't have Nash pick you up and fly you here just to bring me breakfast. What have you got?"

Jonah dumped fries out of a bag and squeezed ketchup onto them. "I've got some background on Claire Forlani and on Dee Atherton. They're mother and daughter."

"You found a birth certificate," Gabe said.

"I found two," Jonah explained. "One in this country for a Claire Forlani. Mother—Susan Forlani, father—Art Forlani. But I couldn't dig up any more information on the parents. No birth certificates on them."

"Which means that whoever established Claire's background cover didn't go very deep," Nicola said.

Jonah met her eyes. "No, they didn't. In fact, other than the birth certificate, a driver's license and a passport which were both issued a year ago, there's no record of Claire Forlani even being in the United States. No college records, no high school records. She's a blank slate."

"I bet I know where you found the other birth certificate," Gabe said.

"Italy," Nicola guessed.

Jonah wrinkled his nose. "Do I get to tell this or not?"

Gabe waved a fry at him. "Go ahead."

"I tried looking in Italy, close to Venice, between 1990 and 1993 because those were the approximate dates you got from your Uncle Ben. And he was right. Dee Atherton had found a partner all right. Claire Forlani was born to Arturo Forlani and Dee Atherton on January 25, 1991. And there are school records there on Claire up until her first year in college. That would be about the same time she turned up in the States with a driver's license and passport."

"So she was raised by her father," Gabe mused. "What have you found on him?"

"According to a business partner of mine in Venice, Arturo Forlani was a respected businessman and a widower until his death a year ago. Claire was his only daughter of record. He didn't speak much English and he didn't travel. Interpol has nothing on him."

"It looks as though Dee Atherton's partner for the museum heist couldn't have been Arturo Forlani," Nicola said.

"I agree," Gabe said.

"Glad it's unanimous," Jonah added.

"Then who was her partner?" Nicola asked. "Bennett said when she met with your father in Venice, she had a partner, one who was excellent at producing forgeries."

"I'm still looking into that," Jonah said. "I've got my friend at Interpol looking for someone who would have been working in Europe during that time period. But I've got nothing back so far."

"My dad's looking for someone working in the States during the past fifteen years," Nicola said.

Gabe set his coffee down. "Nicola thinks the partner might have kept in touch with Claire over the years, perhaps to see if she inherited her mother's talents."

"Not a bad theory." Jonah sent Nicola a smile. "I'll check into it."

Nash wadded up empty wrappers. "What we think we've got is a forger and a security person, two people who combined had a chance to have the same kind of successful career Gabe's father had. And it must have been working because when Dee Atherton had a baby, she left the little girl behind with the father and went back to work." He shot the papers he'd gathered into the waste basket.

"Sixteen years ago—give or take—they came here and Dee sought Gabe's father out to ask for help," Nicola said. "Twice."

"Uncle Ben said she had blueprints. We're assuming she wanted help with breaking through the security of the Denver Art Museum, and the partner who got away was the forger."

"Then Dee was shot and killed, and the partner waited fifteen years to start up again?" Nash asked.

"Not exactly. We think the partner blamed Gabe's father for Dee's death and the failure of the robbery and got part of his or her revenge fifteen years ago." Then she filled Nash and Jonah in on the details of their theory that Raphael Wilder was framed.

"Revenge," Jonah said. "It's a powerful motivator."

"And it seems to have widened beyond my father and me." Gabe filled his friends in on the vandalism at Nicola's apartment and the note.

"So Dee Atherton's partner began his revenge with Gabe's dad and then waited all these years to finish the job?" Nash asked. "He or she had to have been doing something all this time."

Nicola looked at Gabe. "The whole thing about leaving a forgery behind is that it might never be discovered." She rose and began to pace. "Private homes are easier to break into than museums."

"I see where you're going," Jonah said. "You're thinking

the robberies here in Denver may have been going on for a while and the thief has only recently gone public."

"Yes," Nicola said.

"Still, a good forger has to have access to the pieces," Gabe pointed out.

"The Cézanne was on loan to the art museum the first time the attempt was made to steal it. My stepmother might know if the Longfords, the Glastons and the Baileys ever lent their paintings to the museum."

"Call her," Gabe said.

Then it was his own cell phone that rang.

"Wilder," he said. The expression on his face had Nicola's stomach knotting.

"It's Pete," Gabe said, "the young man I stationed at Claire Forlani's door. Someone has made an attempt on her life."

The three men rose at once.

"Wait." Nicola grabbed the towel off her head as she slid off her stool and raced for the stairs. "I need to get dressed."

"We'll wait," Gabe promised.

"Girls," Jonah muttered.

GABE STOOD IN THE HALLWAY directly outside of Claire Forlani's room in the intensive care unit. Once they'd reached the floor, the four of them had split up. Nash and Jonah had remained at the T in the hallway where they could keep the door to the waiting room and both ends of the hallway in view. Nicola had gone to the nurse's station the moment she'd seen that Sid was talking on the phone. He'd moved to talk to his man Pete. The young man had a bandage on his head and he was sitting on a chair on one side of Claire's closed door. A uniformed policeman stood on the other.

Through the glass window, Gabe could see the lights blinking on the machines Claire was hooked up to.

"I'm sorry I let you down, boss," Pete said. "It happened so fast."

"He didn't let you down all by himself."

Gabe switched his gaze to the uniformed officer, a man in his forties with thinning hair.

"The doctors had been through on their morning rounds, the floor was quiet, and I asked Pete if he'd mind covering while I went to get us both some coffee," the older man said. "I should never have left."

"What happened next?" Gabe asked Pete.

"One of the patients coded. The nurse's station cleared," Pete said. "When this guy in scrubs came along pushing a wheelchair, I thought he was here to transport a patient away for some procedure. The next thing I knew, something hit me in the side of my head. Hard. I blacked out for a couple seconds. When I came to and made it into the room, the nurse over there, Sid, was struggling with this guy. I pulled out my gun and told him I'd shoot. He shoved Sid into me and took off."

"It sounds like you did the job I hired you to do," Gabe said, putting a hand on the young man's shoulder. "Sometimes they get away."

"I'd say the two of them did a good job," the uniformed man said. "Sid said that the guy had a pillow over her face when he went in. And your friend here's still a little woozy."

"I'm fine," Pete insisted to the older guy. "Sid checked my eyes. I just need some aspirin."

"I'm familiar with the feeling." Gabe glanced over to where Nicola was talking to Sid. Since he figured she'd get what could be gotten of the young male nurse, he stayed where he was. "What can you tell me about the man who hit you?"

Pete frowned. "He was wearing scrubs—not the plain green ones, the fancier kind that a lot of the nurses wear. He was tall, lean. He was wearing gloves, and he had his hair covered with one of those shower cap things that they wear in the operating rooms on TV shows. He had a mask on, too."

"Could you tell the color of his hair?" Gabe asked.

Pete thought, then shook his head and immediately winced. "Glasses—he was wearing glasses. Black frames."

"Good job." After he gave Pete's shoulder a squeeze, Gabe walked over to where Jonah and Nash stood. "Observations?" he asked.

"It wouldn't be hard to get in here," Jonah said. "As long as you're wearing scrubs and something that could pass for an I.D. badge."

"Not a problem for someone who can copy a Monet or a Cézanne," Nash commented.

Gabe looked back at the room where Claire Forlani lay. "I should have taken more precautions."

"Too bad Nash and I didn't bring our violins to play." Then he met Gabe's eyes. "There were two men on the door. One in your employ and one paid by the city. You were hoping someone would try to contact her. I can't see any way you could have predicted that someone would try to kill her."

"Well, someone definitely did," Gabe said. "Why?"

"My first guess would be to silence her," Jonah said.

"But if this thief framed your father and is now hoping to frame you for revenge, then we have to consider that revenge may also be the motivation here," Nash said.

"She failed to get the statue—therefore, she has to die? If that's true, then Nicola might be the next target."

"Or you," Jonah pointed out.

Gabe turned and when he saw that Nicola was standing at the window of Claire Forlani's room, he joined her and took her hand. Through the glass, the lights on Claire's machines continued to blink.

"According to Pete, her attacker was wearing black-framed glasses and had his or her hair covered. It could be the same person who delivered you the Valentine's Day flowers."

"Yeah. Sid also thinks it may have been a woman."

"Interesting." Keeping her hand in his, he drew her to where Jonah and Nash were waiting. "All we have to do is figure out who and make sure that the Cézanne doesn't get stolen."

"Unless the thief has changed the game plan," Nicola said.

Gabe felt his phone vibrate, took it out, and read the text. "It's from your father. Your stepmother just received a Valentine special delivery card, telling her she'll be relieved of the Cézanne tonight."

"Let's catch a thief," Nicola said.

IT WAS A WORKING LUNCH, but it was the oddest one that Nicola had ever participated in. The cuisine was Chinese takeout, but they'd never made it to the counter in Gabe's kitchen. Instead, she, Gabe, Jonah and Nash had gathered, cartons and chopsticks in hand, around the whiteboard in Gabe's office.

Jonah's contact at Interpol had nothing new. But Marcia had texted Nicola to remind her she was expected to arrive at the house by 5:00 p.m. so that she could dress and stand in the reception line. Her stepmother had also included the information that all three of the French Impressionist paintings stolen so far had been on display at the Denver

Art Museum over the past ten years, as had most of the privately owned art in the Denver area.

"Who else do we need to add to our rogues' gallery?" Gabe asked.

The newspaper articles and photos of the art pieces that had formerly adorned Gabe's whiteboard had been replaced by pictures of everyone who had close access to information about the thefts. Chewing thoughtfully on a piece of Kung Pao chicken, Nicola swept her gaze over them. Mary Thomas and Mark Adams lined the left side of the board. Debra Bancroft, Claire Forlani and Randolph Meyer lined the right-hand side.

While they'd been eating, Gabe and Jonah had run financials on all of them. And they'd come up with nothing suspicious on any of their current suspects. Right now they were thinking of who they might add to the list so they could widen the search.

"I don't think we should add anyone," Nicola said.

"Why not? We've come up dry on these." Jonah offered her some rice, but she waved it on.

"Because, other than Gabe or my father, these are the key figures." She pointed her chopsticks at the board. "They're all close to the case and they all had access to information that would help in the thefts. Anyone we add to the mix like other employees here or at the FBI could play a part in a minor way. But that won't get us any closer to who's behind it."

Gabe set down his carton and moved closer to the board. "She's right. We should be eliminating people instead of adding them. If we're right in thinking the person behind these thefts is Dee Atherton's old partner, then our mastermind can't be Claire. Though she might have a good motive for avenging Dee Atherton's death, she couldn't have been the one to frame my father. Fifteen years ago, she was a child."

"Based on age, we can also eliminate Mark Adams and Randolph Meyer," Nicola said. "That leaves Debra Bancroft and Mary Thomas."

"I hate to rain on this parade," Nash said.

"Liar," Jonah said. "You love to play devil's advocate."

Nash shrugged. "Maybe it's not either of them. Our mastermind may be keeping a low profile. Whoever it is has never shown up on the radar before. And they've managed to keep off of it for the past fifteen years."

Gabe removed the photos of the people they'd eliminated. "Yeah, but there's been a change in the game plan. Once you start delivering announcements and pulling your capers on major holidays, you're putting yourself firmly *on* the radar. I'm betting it's either Mary Thomas or Debra Bancroft."

"Me, too," Nicola said as she slipped her hand into his.

Gabe met her eyes. "If Nicola's right and our forger has spent some of the intervening time creating copies and then secretly breaking into houses and replacing authentic paintings with her work, she's needed inside information on the art collectors here in Denver as well as inside information on their security systems. So if it's between Debra and Mary, the cards are more heavily stacked against Debra. The person who was supposed to break through the security and switch the paintings won't be there, and Debra can get through everything but the last layer."

"We can't eliminate Mary completely because of the forged statue," Nicola said. "The thief had to not only know about its existence but also know where it was."

"I'm leaning toward Debra," Nash said.

"She has my vote." Jonah began to gather up empty cartons. "In any case, we need proof."

Gabe smiled. "That means we'll have to catch her in the act. And I've got a plan."

Jonah placed a hand on Nicola's shoulder. "Make sure you count the girl in. She's smart."

16

"GREAT DRESS," Nash said.

"Yeah." Gabe's eyes shifted immediately to Nicola. She stood with her father and stepmother greeting guests as they entered the salon. Even though he'd been given a preview of the red dress, it still very nearly made his tongue hang out. And the curls were back. Only they looked a lot sexier now than they had when she was ten.

At his side, Nash chuckled. "You've got it bad."

"What are you talking about?" Gabe asked.

"I mention a dress," he waved his glass of champagne. "And there are a lot of them here."

Gabe agreed. They were halfway through the silent auction part of the evening and the stream of viewers through the room had been constant. Currently, the place was glowing with silks and sequins. The scent of expensive perfume mingled with the food that was being offered by uniformed waiters. A string quartet played in one corner. The conversation was muted, and everyone was paying due homage to the Cézanne. Folded slips of paper containing the bids were accumulating in a silver bowl.

"But all I have to do is mention *one* dress and your eyes go directly to Nicola. You're stuck on her."

"Yeah," Gabe agreed as he looked at Nicola again. Each time he did, he felt the impact as if it were the first time.

"Jonah and I like her, for what it's worth."

Gabe shifted his gaze to where his other friend was circulating through the guests offering canapés on a tray. "I'm glad I have your approval."

"Have you told her yet?"

"Told her what?" He felt that same clutch in his stomach he'd felt when Nick Guthrie had been grilling him.

"That you're stuck on her." Nash tipped his glass in the direction of the door. "I wouldn't let the grass grow under your feet. You're not the only one who's impressed with your lady."

Gabe looked back to Nicola and narrowed his eyes when he saw Randolph Meyer raise her hand to his lips.

"Actually, the dress I was originally referring to is on our prime suspect," Nash said.

Gabe shifted his gaze to Debra Bancroft as she circulated through the guests. Her blond hair was smoothed back into a sophisticated twist, and earrings dangled to her shoulders. As far as Debra knew, they were following through on their original plan for tonight. Debra's job was to mingle with the guests while the other members of the G. W. Securities' team were working as waiters just as Jonah was. But Gabe had made a few additions to the plan.

Nash was assigned to keep tabs on Mary Thomas and Randolph Meyer. Both would be seated with him at the Guthries' table. Nicola was assigned to Mark Adams, who was also sitting with the Guthries. And when the wait-staff moved upstairs to serve dinner, Jonah would discard his uniform and return to the salon by way of one of the air ducts where he'd remain until he was needed. Gabe would stay behind in the salon with Debra, and then they would wait.

He didn't have a doubt that Debra would make a move. He'd thought out the various scenarios, and he was pretty sure with Jonah's and Nash's help, he had them covered. Hopefully, his prayer to St. Francis would ensure their success.

"That dress is not off the racks," Nash murmured as they watched Randolph Meyer cross the salon in Debra's direction. "My guess is that it was specifically designed for Ms. Bancroft and for the occasion. Perhaps by our designer friend."

Gabe ran his gaze over the dress again. It was black, sequined, and fell to the floor in a full skirt that swirled around her as she walked. "We know that Meyer designed it specifically for tonight. It wouldn't be difficult to hide a forged painting beneath that skirt."

When he reached her, Randolph Meyer took her hands and kissed them just as he had Nicola's. Debra did not look pleased.

"They look pretty chummy," Nash remarked.

"He may not be the mastermind behind the thefts, but he may have a role to play tonight. Keep very close tabs on him," Gabe murmured.

"On who?" Nicola asked as she joined them.

"Meyer."

Nicola turned to Nash. "I'm here on a mission. There's still a line at the door that goes all the way down the stairs to the foyer. Marcia would like you to start leading the way up to the ballroom for dinner. She wants you to escort Mary Thomas."

"My pleasure, and I'll convince Meyer to come with us," Nash said as he moved away.

As Nicola turned to watch the people, she spoke in a low voice to Gabe. "I'm also supposed to let you know that Dad has nothing to report."

"I recommend the shrimp," Jonah said as he offered them a tray of canapés. "And I do have something. My business partner called to say that the Forlani estate did have a semi-regular visitor over the years, someone who came specifically to visit the daughter, Claire. And I've got a description—tall, blond, attractive."

"Could be Debra," Nicola said. "The clues are piling up, but we need more."

"We'll get it." Gabe let his gaze sweep the room. Debra was checking in with one of the waiters, Mary Thomas was moving toward the door on Nash's arm. Randolph Meyer was following. "You both know what to do," he said.

Jonah moved away.

"Why is it that you and Jonah get to have all the fun while I have to watch over Mark Adams—Mr. Least Likely to Be Involved in this?"

Gabe met her eyes. "*Think* of him as involved. And there may be someone we haven't even thought of. Be careful."

She took his hands and squeezed them. "I'm going to be sitting at a table with Nash and two FBI agents. You may be down here for a time alone with someone who's already tried to kill someone today. Be very careful."

He gripped her hands more tightly when she tried to move away. "Nicola, after this is over, I want some time with you. Maybe we could go away."

She smiled at him, and he felt it again—that punch to the gut. "We're on the same page about that." Then she rose on her toes and brushed her mouth over his. "First, let's catch that thief."

CHANDELIERS GLITTERED, silver gleamed and music floated on the air beneath laughter and the buzz of conversation. Nicola Guthrie had to hand it to her stepmother. Marcia Thorne Guthrie knew how to throw a party. The ballroom at Thorne Mansion had never been this crowded, and from the looks on the faces of the guests, people were having a wonderful time.

The Valentine theme was present, but muted. Red ribbons were tied around small parchment favors that contained a print of the Cézanne. Red sweetheart roses floated in small heart-shaped crystal bowls in the center of each table.

Nearly forty-five minutes had gone by since dinner service had begun. Waiters were clearing the fish course and pouring red wine for the meat course. However, Nicola wanted more than the filet mignon. Time seemed to be dragging. What if they'd been wrong about who the thief was? What if it was someone who hadn't even made their list? Or what if the warning note had been a joke?

But each time the questions entered her mind, they were more than offset by the tingle of anticipation inside of her, which was growing stronger by the second.

Across the round table from her, Nash said something to make Mary Thomas laugh. Mark Adams sat directly to her right, Randolph Meyer to her left, and so far, neither of them had done or said anything in the least suspicious. The only thing she'd picked up was that the two men shared an avid interest in wine and thoroughly approved of the selections Marcia had made for the meal.

She might have joined in their conversation if she hadn't felt so wired. Something was going to happen soon.

As if she'd wished it, the chandeliers flickered overhead and went out. When they came on again, there was a sprinkling of applause. But Mark's voice was very soft and very clear in her ear. "In a few minutes, the lights will go out again, and you'll come with me. Make a noise or try to signal anyone, and Gabe Wilder dies. All I have to do is punch a button on my cell phone."

GABE TURNED TO DEBRA BANCROFT the moment the lights flickered in the salon. She'd glanced up at the overhead chandeliers. But she showed no concern as she shifted her attention back to the Cézanne.

"That's the signal, isn't it, Debra? You installed a timer on the main power switch for the house. Your plan is about to begin."

When she turned to face him, there was an icy coldness in her eyes he'd never seen before. And there was a small caliber gun in her hand. "When did you figure it out?" she asked.

The fact that she didn't attempt to feign innocence told Gabe that his time was short. Jonah would have had time to position himself in the air duct, but there was no way his friend could enter the room without drawing attention to himself.

Gabe figured his best strategy was to throw Debra off balance enough so that he could get the gun or Jonah could enter the room undetected.

"I've suspected ever since the second robbery that some-one here at G. W. had to be involved. But it wasn't until I started working with Nicola that I finally concluded it was you."

Debra frowned. "What could she know? She wasn't even assigned to work on the robberies."

"She was assigned to do research and she came up with the theory that the thief—you—had two goals. To steal the art, specifically the Cézanne, and to ruin me."

"She couldn't have known that."

"She even has a theory about why you want to frame me for the robberies. You made a mistake when you sent Claire Forlani after the St. Francis. She left the forgery behind. That helped us put everything together."

There was a flicker of something in her eyes. Surprise?

Anger? Ego? Then they went cold again, and in the icy depths, Gabe caught his first glimpse of madness.

"I never make mistakes. Never. Other people do. You made the mistake of installing a new alarm system and then letting me see it. I've had time to adjust my plans. You'll have to pay now just like the others."

"Is that what happened to Dee Atherton? She had to pay for her mistakes?"

Gabe noticed the flicker in her eyes again. Definitely surprise this time. "It was the statue that allowed us to connect the dots back to Dee. I know that she came to my father sixteen years ago and that he refused to help her."

"It wasn't the first time he'd refused," she said, the anger clear in her voice. "We'd invited him to join us years ago in Venice and he'd said no because of you. He didn't want to be tied down because he couldn't miss this holiday or that holiday with his son."

"That's why you've scheduled the thefts for holidays. Because my father wanted to spend time with me?"

She smiled and it sent a chill up Gabe's spine. "Yes. I thought it was a nice touch. He used you as an excuse again when we invited him to join us in stealing the Cézanne from the Denver Art Museum. He wouldn't even help Dee with the security. That was his mistake. A fatal one. And Dee made hers when she told me that she could go ahead with the plan without him. She wasn't good enough to pull it off. They both paid."

Gabe stared at her. Why hadn't he seen it before? The coldness in her went so deep. "When Dee set off the alarm, you didn't have time to switch the paintings, so you left her there. You abandoned her. That's why she was shot. And then you framed my father with the Matisse."

"They had to pay. They were keeping me from being all that I can be."

When she glanced at the overhead lights, Gabe was certain that his time was running out. "But it turned out that you couldn't fulfill your potential without a partner after all. Even after you joined G. W. Securities, you couldn't pull off the kind of thefts that you'd pulled with Dee. That's why you visited Claire Forlani in Italy. And when you learned that she'd inherited her mother's talents, you gave her Dee's bracelet and persuaded her to follow in her mother's footsteps."

It wasn't surprise he saw this time, but shock. In spite of that, her gun hand remained steady.

"What I'm not sure I understand is why you tried to kill her. Was it because you feared betrayal? Or maybe you'd begun to sense that she wasn't going to *need* you. She was going to be able to make it on her own. Had she already threatened to leave you after this job?"

Bright spots of color stained Debra's pale cheeks. "No, Claire made a stupid mistake. She was supposed to steal the statue after tonight's robbery. Your signature and fingerprints would be found on it, and that would convince the FBI that you were behind all of the thefts. You'd be arrested and sent to jail, just as your father was. That was the plan."

"A good one," Gabe said as he prayed for time. He wanted to get that gun before the lights went out again. "But once Claire strayed from it, everything started to unravel. You couldn't use her for this job, so you had to come up with an alternate strategy. Then you found a second security system. And whatever your latest plan is, it won't work."

"Yes, it will. Did you think I wouldn't find a way around your system?"

Debra pulled a flashlight out of a pocket in the wide gown of her skirt. "The lights will go out again any second, and they won't come back on. You're going to disarm your new alarm and give me the Cézanne or Nicola Guthrie will be killed."

Fear hit him so hard that for a moment he lost his breath.

The muffled explosion and the blackout occurred at the same instant. Then came the sound of smoke alarms. The only light in the room came from Debra's flashlight and it glinted off her gun.

"I don't believe you have Nicola," Gabe said just as his cell phone vibrated.

"That will be her now." Debra set her flashlight on the small table with the silver bowl and aimed it at the painting. Then she pulled her own cell phone out of a pocket. "Mark Adams has a gun pressed to her gut. Not to her head or her heart. That would be too easy. If the trigger is pulled, she'll bleed out slowly, painfully."

He said a prayer to St. Francis, then spoke into the phone that Debra handed him. "You all right?"

"KEEP YOUR EYES ON ME and everything will be fine," Mark murmured softly.

Nicola badly wanted to glance around the table, to send a signal to Nash or her father. Several minutes had gone by, and the lights hadn't flickered again, but she was very much aware that Mark had his cell phone in his hand. She wasn't sure how much time she had. But her instincts told her that Mark was telling the truth about Gabe.

Even as a waiter set a filet in front of her, she kept her eyes on the agent who had worked so closely with her father. "Why are you doing this?"

His smile was wry. "I was given an offer I couldn't refuse. And the person I work with is very capable."

"Debra Bancroft."

Before Mark Adams could confirm or deny, there was the sound of an explosion. The floor in the ballroom vibrated, the chandeliers chimed. Then the room was pitched into blackness.

Mark's hand grasped her arm. She managed to snag her purse before he pulled her quickly toward the ballroom door. She heard her father's voice, telling everyone to be calm. But she figured Nash would be after her in a flash.

"In here." Mark shoved her into a storage closet right next to the ballroom. She heard the lock click and then felt the press of a gun into her side. "Don't make a sound," he breathed.

She didn't dare. They both heard footsteps running past toward the stairs to the lower floor. The room they were standing in was pitch-black. But she could picture it in her mind. The windowless room was used to store tables, chairs, glassware and china that her stepmother used in the ballroom. Very carefully, she slipped the strap of her purse over her shoulder. She wanted her hands free, and if she got the chance, she would go for her gun.

More footsteps rushed by.

She nearly jumped when Mark pressed a cell phone to her ear.

"Tell Wilder that you're alive and you'll remain that way as long as he does what he's told."

"You all right?" Gabe asked.

"Yes. He has a gun."

Then the line went dead.

17

"YOU WON'T GET AWAY with this, Debra." Gabe kept his voice calm in spite of the fear roiling inside of him. He had to push the image of someone holding Nicola at gunpoint out of his mind.

"I will with your help. Or Nicola Guthrie dies. Right now. All I have to do is punch one number into my cell."

"Why don't you fill me in on your plan? I'll be of more help if I'm not operating blind."

"Or you'll be more prepared to stop me. Turn off the second layer of security and get the Cézanne out of its frame. No tricks."

Gabe stepped closer to the glass case, pressed his thumb against the keypad and punched in a code. "I have to have some guarantee that Nicola Guthrie will be safe."

The glass slid open and Debra stared at it. "It's voice activated. I figured that much. But what else?"

"A certain combination of words." And he could lock the painting up again just as easily.

"Don't even think of saying them again. Just get it out of the frame. We don't have much time."

Gabe couldn't have agreed with her more. Time was not working in his favor. Jonah couldn't make a move, not with Nicola being held hostage. And once he handed the painting over to Debra, he would have nothing to bargain with.

"NOW WHAT?" Nicola whispered. She felt Mark ease away from the door. From the sound of his breathing, she knew that he was standing across from her. The gun was no longer pressed to her side, but it was close. No more than a foot or two separated them in the narrow room. She formed a mental picture of him in her mind.

"As soon as she signals me that she has the painting, we'll leave. That explosion you heard set off a fire in the kitchen area. They're already evacuating the ballroom, and we'll slip out with the others. As long as we have you and Wilder as hostages, they're not going to stop us."

The plan sounded good on the surface. And Mark might even take her along. But Debra wouldn't be taking Gabe. Once she had the painting, she'd kill Gabe and take off on her own.

Ruthlessly, Nicola pushed back the surge of fear. It wasn't going to help her a bit to keep thinking about how much danger Gabe might be in. She had to concentrate on Mark Adams. He was her only chance of improving Gabe's chances.

"You've surprised me, Mark. We suspected that someone in the FBI office might be involved, but I didn't think it was you. You're a family man."

His short laugh held no humor. "Used to be. My family is breaking up. My ex-wife is about to remarry and start a new life. Debra has helped me through a rough time. With the money we've made on these robberies, we'll also be able to start a new life."

His belief in Debra was very strong in his voice. Nicola figured her best strategy was to chip away at that trust.

"What's taking so long? Debra has to have the painting by now. She's not going to call you."

"Shut up."

"She's going to leave you behind." In her mind, Nicola tried to imagine exactly where Mark's gun was. She pictured his height and exactly where the angle of his elbow would be. "If you kill me, there's no way you'll get away with it. My father will hunt you down. If you stop now, you can make a deal."

"She's going to call."

"No. She's going to cut her losses. That's the way she operates. Do you know that this isn't her first string of robberies? She's been at it for twenty years or more and she's never gotten caught."

"You're lying."

"She's good—so good she's never even made it onto Interpol's or the FBI's radar screen. No wonder you let her dupe you. There's a good chance she's been stealing art here in Denver ever since she went to work for G. W. Securities. That means she's got money tucked away. And so far the people she takes on as partners end up dead. This morning she tried to kill Claire Forlani in her hospital room."

"That's not true."

But the quaver in his voice was just what she'd been waiting for. In a very quick move, she lunged for his gun hand and used all her weight to shove it aside. There was a deafening explosion as she brought her knee up hard into his groin.

The instant she felt him slump, she let go of his arm, unlocked the door and raced out into the hallway.

Guests were still poring out of the ballroom. She pushed past them. At the top of the stairs, she spotted her father on the landing.

"Gabe," she shouted at him. But he couldn't hear her above the noise of the crowd. And they were slowing her down.

Taking out her cell, she punched in Gabe's number. It rang, then rang again. *Pick it up. Pick it up. St. Francis, make him pick it up.*

"It's taken you long enough to get it out of the frame. Now roll it up."

Gabe did, taking as much time as he dared. When his cell vibrated, he reached to take the call.

"Keep your hands on the painting where I can see them," Debra said.

"It's my cell. It could be Nick Guthrie, Nash or Jonah. If I don't answer, they'll check here first."

"Okay, but watch what you say."

Gabe didn't have to say anything. He wasn't sure he could when he heard Nicola's voice.

"I'm okay. Take her down."

Then he drew in a deep breath and, shoving the painting back into the case, he said, "Nicola Guthrie is safe."

The glass slid shut.

"No. Make it open again." There was a thread of panic in her voice, but she kept her eyes on him, her gun steady as she pressed a number into her phone.

For a moment, Gabe let the silence stretch between them. "She got away. Nicola's safe."

"No." The coldness was gone from her voice. In its place was fury. "I want the painting."

In the glow of the flashlight, Gabe saw her hand was still steady on the gun.

"No," Gabe said.

The lights came on, and Gabe could see that there was

more than anger in her eyes. There was also a trace of madness.

In his peripheral vision, he saw the door to the salon open. Framed in it, Nick Guthrie and Nash stood, their guns aimed at Debra. And over her shoulder, he saw Jonah lift the grate aside and crawl out of the air duct.

"Drop the gun, Debra," Nick Guthrie said.

"No. You drop yours or I'll kill him. I'll blow his head off."

"You'll still be dead," Nicola said, stepping into the space between her father and Nash. "If you want to take someone with you, why don't you take me? I got away from Mark. I'm the one who spoiled your plan."

"You." Debra screamed the word as she swung the gun.

Gabe leapt forward. There was gunfire, a flurry of movement. Then Debra was lying beneath him on the floor, not moving.

He lifted his head to scan the room for Nicola. She was flat on the floor, Nash on top of her. But her eyes were on him.

"You all right?" she asked.

"Yeah. You?"

"Yes." Nash assisted her to her feet.

Gabe rolled off of Debra. Her blood stained his shirt. Jonah was checking for a pulse.

"She's breathing," he said. "Looks like a shoulder wound."

Gabe got to his feet, drew Nicola into his arms and simply held on. "She nearly shot you."

"She nearly shot *you*."

"Well," Nash said. "You're even then. Seems to me that the big mistake Debra made was tangling with either one of you."

As soon as Nick Guthrie finished talking with the rest of his team and calling for an ambulance, he joined Nash and Jonah near the Cézanne.

Still keeping his arm around Nicola to hold her close, Gabe met Guthrie's eyes. "Mark Adams?"

"He's in custody. After Nicola got away, he couldn't wait to turn himself in. He wants a deal. But I'm not feeling particularly generous. He tried to kill my daughter."

"Yeah."

"Well, he didn't succeed," Nicola pointed out.

"No, he didn't. I owe St. Francis for that one," Gabe said.

"Not just St. Francis." Nick Guthrie moved to pull Nicola into his arms for a long hug. When he released her, he said, "In this case, St. Francis had some help. You knew just what to say to distract her. My heart stopped beating when she swung her gun in your direction, but it gave us a chance to take her down. Good job."

"Thanks. Does that mean that you're going to let me work in the field?"

He studied her for a moment. "I'm going to need to replace Mark Adams. I can't think of a better candidate for the job than you."

Nicola was still hugging her father when the medics appeared at the door.

As they watched Debra being loaded onto a stretcher, Jonah said, "You know, Gabe used Nicola's name to open the glass case," Jonah said.

"Really?" Nick Guthrie asked.

Jonah nodded. "First and last names. He said them twice, and both times the glass moved.

"I've tried to tell him he's really stuck on her," Nash said.

Nicola looked into Gabe's eyes. "You used my name as the code?"

He framed her face with his hands. "Your name was what was in my mind while I was working on the system. For three months, I haven't been able to get you out of my head."

Then he pulled her close and simply held on for a very long time. There'd been that instant of helplessness he'd felt when Debra had swung her gun toward Nicola. For just that brief span of time, he'd felt the same way he'd felt when each of his parents had died.

As if she understood, Nicola ran her hands up and down his back. "I'm here," she murmured. "And so are you."

IT WAS WELL AFTER MIDNIGHT when Gabe and Nicola walked into his apartment. Debra Bancroft was in the hospital in stable condition. They were right about the forgery being concealed beneath her gown. Mark Adams had called a lawyer but was still hoping for a deal. Marcia had managed to resuscitate the chef after the filet mignon course had been ruined so that he could serve desserts and cognac in the ballroom. When they'd left Thorne Mansion, her father had been sharing some of his single malt Scotch with Nash and Jonah in his office.

"I wonder who the new owner of the Cézanne is," Nicola said. "In all the excitement, I forgot to ask."

"Your father told me that they received the highest bid that's ever been made this year. And it came from the Robineau family. It seems they couldn't bear to part with the painting."

"Nice." She tried for a smile and then yawned.

"You're tired," he said as he tucked a curl behind her ear.

"And you're not?"

"Yes, but I wanted…we haven't had any time together. I thought… Are you too tired for a nightcap?"

He was nervous, Nicola realized. And she'd never before seen him that way. "Do you happen to have a white wine in that magic cooler of yours?"

"I do." He moved away to select a bottle and uncork it. She followed and climbed onto a stool at the counter.

"I got some good news from Pete at the hospital while you were saying goodbye to your stepmother. Claire Forlani regained consciousness for a short time. The doctors believe she's going to recover fully."

"Good. I'm going to see if I can talk Marcia into hiring a defense team for her."

"You're going to what?" He turned to stare at her.

"Marcia likes to do that kind of thing. She's very generous with her time and with her money. And who knows what kinds of lies Debra Bancroft told that girl about her mother. She's so young. Maybe you could hire her at G. W. Securities."

"And you accused me of being a caregiver." He handed her a glass of wine. "I didn't even get you a Valentine gift."

"Good. One bouquet was enough."

Though she got a smile out of him, he didn't laugh. Instead, he lifted his glass in a toast. "To your new job. You got what you wanted."

She touched her glass to his and sipped. She had gotten what she wanted, a chance to work at her father's side. But as she looked into Gabe's eyes, she knew that it was no longer all she wanted. She was looking right at what she wanted more than anything.

She drew in a breath and let it out. She was no longer the Nicola who just worked hard and waited for things to happen. So in spite of the nerves tightening in her own stomach, she said, "You have something that you want to talk about. What?"

Fear. It danced up his spine. And it was every bit as sharp as what he'd felt when he'd thought Debra was going to shoot her. "I need time with you."

She raised her brows. "I thought we already agreed on that. We're going away. You can choose our destination. I have some vacation time."

"No." He set his glass down and ran his hands through his hair. "I want more than a vacation. I want…" He turned away, paced to the counter, then turned back to face her. "I stayed away from you for three months. I wasted all that time. That was my fault. And then I very nearly lost you tonight. That was my fault, too."

Nicola frowned at him. "And why was either of those things your fault?" She set down her wine and held up a finger. "Number one, I think it was St. Francis who was responsible for keeping us apart for three months."

He cocked his head to one side studying her. "How do you figure?"

"Father Mike said the statue was playing a part in all of this. If we hadn't run into each other in the church, if I hadn't been sure you were someone else, if we hadn't made love, we might not be where we are right now."

"And Debra might not have nearly killed you tonight. At least you can't argue that I'm not responsible for that. I hired her. I put her in a position to do everything she did."

She slipped off her stool, rounded the counter and grabbed his face in her hands. "Look at me. Debra Bancroft is crazy."

"Yes. She was with me for five years, and I didn't see it."

"She was crazier for a lot longer than that, and she was good at hiding it. Look at how many lives she ruined—your father's, Dee Atherton's, Mark Adams', Claire's and she very nearly ruined yours. How do you think I felt when I was stuck in that closet with Mark? I knew that the second you gave her the Cézanne, she was going to kill you."

Gabe pulled her into his arms and held on tight. "I've never been that afraid before."

"Well, the feeling was mutual. And you're really going to have to work on this 'I can protect everyone' gene."

He drew back and looked into her eyes. "And you're not guilty of the same? Who's going to see that Claire Forlani gets a defense team?"

With a sigh, he rested his forehead on hers.

"Maybe we can work on it together," she said.

"Yeah. But it's going to be a big job. It's going to take a lot of time."

"Eons," she agreed. "And there are other things, too. We both have very demanding jobs. We'll have to work on making time for each other."

"I do consulting work for the FBI. Maybe we could work together again."

"I'd like that." She met his eyes, saw the gleam in his. "Ready?"

"For what?"

"A lifetime of very hard work." She smiled at him. "And fun?"

"Yeah." He wound one of her curls around his finger. "What about you?"

"Very ready. And now will you please take me to bed?"

Laughing, he scooped her up into his arms and headed toward the stairs. "I thought you'd never ask."

"I didn't have to the first time." She nipped on his lower lip.

"Neither did I."

"Something else we'll have to work on," she said as they tumbled onto the bed.

"Forever."

* * * * *

*Be sure to look for Nash's story
coming in July as part of the
UNIFORMLY HOT! miniseries.*

♦ Harlequin® *Blaze*™

COMING NEXT MONTH
Available February 22, 2011

#597 FACE-OFF
Encounters
Nancy Warren

#598 IN THE LINE OF FIRE
Uniformly Hot!
Jennifer LaBrecque

#599 IN GOOD HANDS
Kathy Lyons

#600 INEVITABLE
Forbidden Fantasies
Michelle Rowen

#601 HIGH OCTANE
Texas Hotzone
Lisa Renee Jones

#602 PRIMAL CALLING
Jillian Burns

USA TODAY *bestselling author Lynne Graham*
is back with a thrilling new trilogy
SECRETLY PREGNANT, CONVENIENTLY WED

Three heroines must marry alpha males to keep
their dreams...but Alejandro, Angelo and Cesario
are not about to be tamed!

Book 1—JEMIMA'S SECRET
Available March 2011 from Harlequin Presents®.

JEMIMA yanked open a drawer in the sideboard to find
Alfie's birth certificate. Her son was her husband's child.
It was a question of telling the truth whether she liked it or
not. She extended the certificate to Alejandro.

"This has to be nonsense," Alejandro asserted.

"Well, if you can find some other way of explaining how
I managed to give birth by that date and Alfie not be yours,
I'd like to hear it," Jemima challenged.

Alejandro glanced up, golden eyes bright as blades and
as dangerous. "All this proves is that you must still have
been pregnant when you walked out on our marriage. It
does not automatically follow that the child is mine."

"'I know it doesn't suit you to hear this news now and I
really didn't want to tell you. But I can't lie to you about it.
Someday Alfie may want to look you up and get acquainted."

"If what you have just told me is the truth, if that little
boy does prove to be mine, it was vindictive and extremely
selfish of you to leave me in ignorance!"

Jemima paled. "When I left you, I had no idea that I was
still pregnant."

"Two years is a long period of time, yet you made no
attempt to inform me that I might be a father. I will want
DNA tests to confirm your claim before I make any deci-

sion about what I want to do."

"Do as you like," she told him curtly. "*I* know who Alfie's father is and there has never been any doubt of his identity."

"I will make arrangements for the tests to be carried out and I will see you again when the result is available," Alejandro drawled with lashings of dark Spanish masculine reserve.

"I'll contact a solicitor and start the divorce," Jemima proffered in turn.

Alejandro's eyes narrowed in a piercing scrutiny that made her uncomfortable. "It would be foolish to do anything before we have that DNA result."

"I disagree," Jemima flashed back. "I should have applied for a divorce the minute I left you!"

Alejandro quirked an ebony brow. "And why didn't you?"

Jemima dealt him a fulminating glance but said nothing, merely moving past him to open her front door in a blunt invitation for him to leave.

"I'll be in touch," he delivered on the doorstep.

What is Alejandro's next move? Perhaps rekindling their marriage is the only solution! But will Jemima agree?

Find out in Lynne Graham's
exciting new romance
JEMIMA'S SECRET

Available March 2011
from Harlequin Presents®.

Start your Best Body today with these top 3 nutrition tips!

1. **SHOP THE PERIMETER OF THE GROCERY STORE:** The good stuff—fruits, veggies, lean proteins and dairy—always line the outer edges of the store. When you veer into the center aisles, you enter the temptation zone, where the unhealthy foods live.

2. **WATCH PORTION SIZES:** Most portion sizes in restaurants are nearly twice the size of a true serving and at home, it's easy to "clean your plate." Use these easy serving guidelines:
   - Protein: the palm of your hand
   - Grains or Fruit: a cup of your hand
   - Veggies: the palm of two open hands

3. **USE THE RAINBOW RULE FOR PRODUCE:** Your produce drawers should be filled with every color of fruits and vegetables. The greater the variety, the more vitamins and other nutrients you add to your diet.

Find these and many more helpful tips in

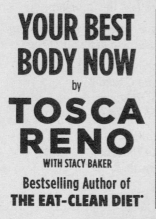

YOUR BEST BODY NOW
by
TOSCA RENO
WITH STACY BAKER

Bestselling Author of
THE EAT-CLEAN DIET®

Available wherever books are sold!

HARLEQUIN®
Super Romance

Top author
Janice Kay Johnson
brings readers a riveting new romance
with

Bone Deep

Kathryn Riley is the prime suspect in
the case of her husband's disappearance
four years ago—that is, until someone tries
to make her disappear…forever. Now
handsome police chief Grant Haller must
stop suspecting Kathryn and instead begin
to protect her. But can Grant put aside the
growing feelings for Kathryn long enough
to catch the real criminal?

Find out in March.

*Available wherever
books are sold.*

HARLEQUIN *Presents*

USA TODAY *Bestselling Author*

Lynne Graham

is back with her most exciting trilogy yet!

SECRETLY PREGNANT
CONVENIENTLY WED

Jemima, Flora and Jess aren't looking for love,
but all have babies very much in mind...and they may
just get their wish and more with the wealthiest, most
handsome and impossibly arrogant men in Europe!

Coming March 2011

JEMIMA'S SECRET

Alejandro Navarro Vasquez has long desired vengeance after
his wife, Jemima, betrayed him. When he discovers the
whereabouts of his runaway wife—and that she has a two-
year-old son—Alejandro is determined to settle the score....

FLORA'S DEFIANCE (April 2011)
JESS'S PROMISE (May 2011)

Available exclusively from Harlequin Presents.

www.eHarlequin.com

HP12975